So that was the "Mac" MacKenzie,

the hospital hunk who was known far and wide throughout the county for his bedside manner. Jolene smiled to herself as she turned away. She could spot his type a mile away. He was a player.

In the next moment, the rear section of the emergency room was filled with another emergency.

"Kind of like when the Native Americans attacked the covered wagons in the old Westerns, isn't it?" Dr. Mac said.

As the comment came from behind her, a shiver danced down Jolene's neck and shoulders. Was he standing right on top of her? Jolene gave him a disparaging look before attending to a patient.

"Have I offended you somehow?" Mac asked.

"I don't think this is the time to hit on me, Doctor," Jolene told him crisply as she hurried away.

Mac was speechless. He'd been put in his place royally. Put in his place within a tiny, obscure box and had the lid slammed down on him. Tight.

His interest was seriously piqued....

Dear Reader,

Have you ever been so excited after reading a book that you're bursting to talk about it with others? That's exactly how I feel after reading many of the superb stories that the talented authors from Silhouette Special Edition deliver time and again. And I'm delighted to tell you about Readers' Ring, our exciting new book club. These books are designed to help you get others together to discuss the brilliant and involving romance novels you come back for month after month.

Bestselling author Sherryl Woods launches the promotion with *Ryan's Place* (#1489), in which the oldest son of THE DEVANEYS learns that he was abandoned by his parents and separated from his brothers—a shocking discovery that only a truly strong woman could help him get through! Be sure to check out the discussion questions at the end of the novel to help jump-start reading group discussions.

Also, don't miss the other five keepers we're offering this month: *Willow in Bloom* by Victoria Pade (#1490); *Big Sky Cowboy* by Jennifer Mikels (#1491); *Mac's Bedside Manner* by Marie Ferrarella (#1492); *Hers To Protect* by Penny Richards (#1493); and *The Come-Back Cowboy* by Jodi O'Donnell (#1494).

Please send me your comments about the Readers' Ring and what you like or dislike about what you're seeing in the line.

Happy reading!

Karen Taylor Richman,
Senior Editor

Please address questions and book requests to:
Silhouette Reader Service
U.S.: 3010 Walden Ave., P.O. Box 1325, Buffalo, NY 14269
Canadian: P.O. Box 609, Fort Erie, Ont. L2A 5X3

Marie Ferrarella

MAC'S BEDSIDE MANNER

Silhouette

SPECIAL EDITION™

Published by Silhouette Books

America's Publisher of Contemporary Romance

To Patience Smith,
Welcome aboard

SILHOUETTE BOOKS

ISBN 0-373-24492-4

MAC'S BEDSIDE MANNER

Visit Silhouette at www.eHarlequin.com

Printed in U.S.A.

Books by Marie Ferrarella in Miniseries

MARIE FERRARELLA

earned a master's degree in Shakespearean comedy, and, perhaps as a result, her writing is distinguished by humor and natural dialogue. This RITA® Award-winning author's goal is to entertain and to make people laugh and feel good. She has written over one hundred books for Silhouette, some under the name Marie Nicole. Her romances are beloved by fans worldwide and have been translated into Spanish, Italian, German, Russian, Polish, Japanese and Korean.

What's Happening to

Bachelor #1:
Lukas Graywolf + Lydia Wakefield
= Together Forever
IN GRAYWOLF'S HANDS (SIM #1155)

Bachelor #2:
Dr. Reese Bendenetti + London Merriweather
= True Love
M.D. MOST WANTED (SIM #1167)

Bachelor #3:
Dr. Harrison MacKenzie + Nurse Jolene DeLuca
= Matrimonial Bliss
MAC'S BEDSIDE MANNER (SSE #1492)

Bachelor #4:
Dr. Terrance McCall + Dr. Alix Duncan
= ???
The fall of Dr. McCall will occur in
Silhouette Intimate Moments, December 2002

Chapter One

There was no doubt about it, Harrison MacKenzie thought. He was one very lucky man.

Mac walked down the corridor past Blair Memorial's MRI lab. He nodded at a hospital administrator he recognized by sight, though not by name. He knew he was one of the fortunate ones. He liked what he did for a living and he was good at it. Very good.

His skill wasn't an overstated, overblown egotistical assessment of his capabilities; it was simply a given, a fact. He made sure of it. There was no excuse for seeking middle ground or being content with half measures. Mac didn't believe in riding on yesterday's accolades, of which there were more than a few. Yesterday's accolades wouldn't help today's patient, or tomorrow's.

And that was his business, his passion: Helping today's patient.

He stopped a moment at the vending machine, feeding it quarters in order to feed his own sweet tooth. A small dark chocolate bar did a high dive from its position on the rack, surrendering itself to the inevitable. Mac retrieved it and peeled back the wrapper with relish. He'd never gotten over his love of chocolate.

The people who came to him carried baggage—hidden or in plain sight—that when unpacked ultimately contained some sort of crisis of self-esteem. Large or small, the content was always the same. Quite literally, they needed his help to face the world, needed him to rid them of some superficial flaw that had managed to get the better of them and interfered with their daily lives.

Never mind that they might be people of worth beneath their skins, they needed this badge, this emblem, this shield that he could give them through the skillful manipulation of his scalpel. All this in order to feel better about themselves.

So to the very apex of his ability, Mac gave it to them and let the magic of change do the rest. For his talent, he collected a very sizable fee.

The children were another matter.

The children he operated on came to him broken, scarred, either from birth or through some kind of horrific accident. Those were the cases that both broke his heart and buoyed his spirit. Because he could help. In some fashion, some manner, he could help. He made sure of that.

And he gave a piece of himself to everyone. Because he remembered Carrie.

Remembered his effervescent older sister and how

after the car accident, the very light within her eyes had disappeared, like a candle being blown out by the wind. It had happened the night after the prom. The windshield had shattered, sending glass flying everywhere. Large shards had slashed one side of her face like a rapier, disfiguring her.

Traumatized, Carrie withdrew from the world and, most hurtfully, from him. She chose instead to exist behind her scars like a wounded animal imprisoned by circumstances, unable to free herself of the shackles fate had imposed and she had reinforced. Shame changed her from the outgoing, loving young woman she was to someone he didn't begin to know. Eventually, when there was enough money to pay the fees, it was the unrelenting efforts of a plastic surgeon that had set Carrie free and returned her to the world of the living.

It was the kind of a difference he wanted to make. The kind of difference, Mac liked to think, that he *did* make. It didn't matter if the families of the children could pay. He was paid in currency far dearer than paper or coin could ever be. His payment was the genuine smile of a child when he or she first looked in the mirror and truly liked what they saw.

Crumpling the wrapper, Mac tossed it into a wastebasket as he turned the corner. Reflexes had him coming to a skidding halt, narrowly avoiding an unintentional christening of his newly purchased shoes.

Jorge Ruiz plunged his mop into the bucket, dragging the latter back into a safety zone. The smile he flashed was neither sheepish nor apologetic, bordering instead on the amused.

"Sorry, Dr. Mac, you on duty today?" the ebony

skinned orderly asked mechanically, knowing the answer before it was given. Jorge knew everything there was to know about the operation of one of Southern California's most respected hospitals.

Mac nodded, then looked at his watch. "For another five minutes, Jorge, and then I'm off."

It was Wednesday, known far and wide to a host of doctors as their unofficial day off. Mac's observance of the day entailed keeping his office closed, but he still put in an E.R. shift, one of two he did on a weekly basis. He did more when a space needed covering.

Wednesdays was also the day when he liked to schedule most of his more difficult operations.

However, today had turned out to be incredibly light. His last patient had been seen to three hours ago, heavily bruised but now in possession of a new, far more delicate nose. The E.R. was quieter than a stadium two hours after a championship game had been lost, and Mac was looking forward to taking out Lynda Rogers, a curvaceous pharmaceutical representative for the Tyler & Rice Drug Company. He'd run into her at the beginning of the week when they'd shared a stuck elevator for the space of twenty-five minutes.

The ordeal had been far from unpleasant. Lynda, it had turned out, had a fear of small places and had literally clung to him for the duration of the elevator's immobility. By the time it was running again, he'd gotten all her vital statistics, half her family history and knew he had an exciting evening ahead of him once they got together.

Which by his watch was in a little over four hours.

"Heads up, people," Wanda Hanlon, the formidable-looking head nurse, called out as she replaced the receiver in its cradle and came around from behind the centrally located desk. At six-one, Wanda had a commanding presence the moment she entered a scene. Her booming voice did nothing to negate that impression. "We've got a crowd coming in." She frowned, shaking her salt-and-pepper head.

"Some party-goers tried to see how many of them could fit on a balcony. The fools got up to twenty-three before the whole thing just collapsed under their weight."

"Damn." Jorge whistled and leaned on his mop, amused. "What makes people so stupid?"

"In this case, probably more than their share of cheap wine."

The comment, stated in a soft voice that made Mac think of a silk scarf being lightly slipped along bare skin, came from behind him.

Turning, he saw a petite nurse with short, straight blond hair and flashing green eyes. She looked as if she had to place rocks in her pockets to keep from being blown away whenever the annual Santa Ana winds swept in from the California desert. At six-four, he could have easily walked right into her and not noticed unless he was deliberately looking down.

Mac's mouth curved in appreciation. The woman didn't smile in response.

First time that had happened, he thought.

"Not a very charitable attitude," he observed.

The nurse spared him a half shrug. "No, but probably an accurate one."

Aware that Jorge was taking this all in as if it were

a spectator sport played out for his benefit, Mac opened his mouth to say something else, but the woman was already walking away as if he hadn't even been there.

That surprised him even more. Her attention appeared riveted to the rear doors that would spring open any second, ushering in gurneys bearing wounded cargo.

Bemused, Mac shifted his gaze to Jorge. "And who was that little bright ray of sunshine?"

Jorge had been at Blair ever since it first opened its doors nearly thirty years ago. Unofficially he was known as the go-to man, an eternal source of information. He was also the man who could mysteriously come up with things that Administration maintained couldn't be obtained for a variety of reasons and certainly not without a mountain of paperwork. Reasons never stopped Jorge, and paperwork was something that never obstructed his path. Mac had come to regard the man as nothing short of a national treasure.

"Pretty little thing," Jorge agreed. Two even rows of gleaming white teeth reinforcing the pleasure he received from observing the woman. "Her name's Jolene DeLuca. Fresh from San Francisco General. Divorced. Has a two-year-old daughter named Amanda. Lives near her mother, Erika. Erika's a widow."

Amused, Mac asked. "What's her shoe size?"

Jorge kept a straight face. "Dunno, but I'm working on it."

Mac shook his head in pure delight. "Tell me, Jorge, is there anything that goes on in this place that you don't know?"

Jorge didn't even pretend to think the question

over. "Nope." Eyes the color of midnight met Mac's. "You wouldn't be asking me if you thought I didn't know."

"You're right, I wouldn't. Thanks for the Cliff's Notes." Mac turned away, about to head in the direction of the rear doors.

"Oh, Dr. Mac, one more thing," Jorge called after him. Mac looked at him over his shoulder, one brow raised in silent query. "Nurse DeLuca doesn't much care for doctors."

"Then she's in the wrong profession." Although that would explain the frosty shoulder, Mac decided. It was a condition, he was confident, that would change in the very near future. He'd never met a frosty shoulder he couldn't warm up. Grinning, Mac gave the older man a two-finger salute. "Thanks, I'll keep that in mind."

Jorge went back to cleaning up the mess that had been left by a nine-year-old. The latter had discovered a neglected Easter basket filled with six-month-old, slightly melted chocolate and had decided to consume the entire contents in one sitting rather than share it with his older sister.

Mac noted that the nurse with the frosty attitude had sought out Wanda's company. Probably thought she was "safe" there, he mused as he approached her.

By all rights, he knew he was free to go home and if he moved quickly, he could make good his escape before any of the ambulances arrived with the inebriated party-goers. But the world of medicine wasn't something he chose to escape. He hadn't worked damn hard to become a doctor just to shirk off the mantle at will. Being a doctor didn't end the moment his shift was over or when he exited through the hospital's electronic doors.

As far as he was concerned, being a doctor was like his being of Scottish descent. It was a twenty-four-hour deal. He was a Scotsman waking and sleeping. The same could be said of his being a physician. That meant helping whenever he could.

The rear doors flew open.

He was on.

So that was him, Jolene thought, walking away from the two men and toward the hospital's rear doors. That was great Dr. Harrison MacKenzie, known far and wide throughout the county for his bedside manner. Both in and out of the hospital, to hear Rebecca Wynters tell it. And tell it and tell it.

Jolene smiled to herself. Rebecca was the reason she'd gotten this position at Blair in the first place, so she couldn't be too hard on the woman. And besides, Rebecca was her friend, her very good friend. They went all the way back to third grade together.

Although at times, when Jolene thought of the romantic entanglements her friend got into, it seemed as if Rebecca hadn't acquired any more brains since they played on the swings together in the schoolyard. She still fell for looks and forgot to factor in anything else—like character.

But then, she supposed on the plus side, Rebecca didn't have a bad marriage behind her. Just a string of relationships that didn't work out. Like the one with Dr. Wonderful. Although to hear Rebecca tell it—and she did—the tall plastic surgeon still owned that title. Rebecca had gone out with Harrison

MacKenzie several times and had nothing but breath-less words to say about him, even after they stopped seeing each other. Her eyes seemed to glow whenever she mentioned his name.

Jolene shook her head. Some people never learned.

However, that group didn't, fortunately, include her. As far as she was concerned, Dr. Harrison MacKenzie was a player. She could spot one a mile away now.

Too bad her eyesight hadn't been that good before she'd gotten involved with Matt and put him through school, she thought.

But then, she wouldn't have had Amanda. Her little girl was worth any humiliation Jolene had had to en-dure. Like finding her husband breaking in his new couch after office hours with his squeaky voiced, mammary gland endowed receptionist.

Straw that broke the camel's back, Jolene thought ruefully. At least her experience with Matt had taught her well. And if it hadn't, her three years at San Fran-cisco General would have. Doctors thought them-selves a breed apart from the rest of humanity. The rules of society didn't apply to them except when they wanted them to. They certainly believed themselves to be two cuts above the nurses they dealt with. And she was first and foremost a nurse, the way her mother had been before her and her grandmother before that.

It was what she was, Jolene thought as she watched the doors and waited for them to spring open, and what she would always be.

If she didn't have Amanda to provide and care for, Jolene would have opted to go work in a third world country where her dedication and knowledge would have been truly appreciated and there wouldn't have been a host of overbearing doctors to deal with. Just perhaps one within a thousand-mile radius.

Her grandmother had been such a dedicated woman in her youth, selflessly giving herself up to the hard life found in underdeveloped regions in Africa. She'd been a Red Cross nurse when her grandfather had met her.

Jolene smiled to herself. Her grandfather had been the one doctor that was the exception to her rule.

Just then, the rear doors burst open.

The next moment, the rear section of the emergency room was filled with the sight, sounds and smell of what had been a near fatal disaster.

"Kind of like when the Native Americans attacked the covered wagons in the old Westerns, isn't it?"

The comment came from directly behind her. A shiver danced down her neck and shoulder blades in response to the whiff of warm breath that accompanied his words.

What was he, standing right on top of her?

Turning almost all the way around, Jolene saw that Rebecca's knight in tarnished armor had somehow gotten directly behind her without her noticing. Served her right for letting her thoughts wander.

Jolene turned back toward the incoming gurneys a split second after giving the man a disparaging look.

"Except that we're supposed to help them, not shoot at them," she retorted icily.

Nurses and doctors were pairing themselves off, bracketing gurneys and the attendants that came in with them. Mac paused just long enough to look quizzically at the nurse with the killer body. "Have I offended you somehow?"

"I don't think now's the time to hit on me, Doctor," she told him crisply. She was already hurrying away from him. "We have work to do."

For a moment Mac was speechless. He'd been put in his place royally. Put in his place within a tiny, obscure box and had the lid slammed down on him. Tight.

His interest was seriously piqued.

But interest was going to have to wait. Though gifted at multitasking from an early age, Mac gave the emergency situation his entire focus. He fell into place beside the fourth gurney as it came through the doors and began shooting questions at the young female paramedic closest to him.

For the next hour, it felt as if someone had unleashed a dam. An endless stream of injured partygoers kept coming and coming. Each time it seemed as if that had been the last of them, another ambulance arrived, bearing another casualty.

"What are we, the only hospital in the area?" one of the doctors who had been called down groused.

Overhearing as she hurried to another bed, Wanda answered, "We're the only ones whose trauma area is equipped to handle this kind of volume. Dr. Mac, they need you in Trauma Room Three," she called out.

Mac looked at the nurse practitioner working with him on a twenty-year-old woman who seemed to have every part of her body pierced with something. The piercing in her thigh hadn't been of her choice. He and Martha had worked for over ten minutes, making sure the wound the vocal party-goer had sustained wouldn't begin to gush again. It appeared to be stable.

"Go ahead," Martha urged. "I can handle this. It's all over but the shouting."

Considering that the young woman they were working on was hurling four-letter words at them regarding the man who'd thrown the party, Mac thought it rather an apt description of the situation.

"I'm all yours," he told Wanda, hurrying behind her.

"Be still my heart," the woman quipped, covering her ample chest with a rubber gloved hand. She brought Mac to a man, who looked as if he'd been on the bottom of the pile in the pyramid after the balcony's collapse.

This, Mac quickly assessed, was going to take more than simple suturing and cleaning.

Someone brushed against his elbow in the tight space around the gurney and as he automatically looked, his eyes met the new nurse's.

"How are you holding up?" he asked.

She seemed to take the question as an affront to her abilities. "Fine."

Mac felt as if he'd just been fired on at point-blank range.

He looked at Wanda, who shrugged in response to his silent question. She didn't seem to know what was wrong with the new nurse, either.

For the following three and a half hours, Mac found himself hip deep in sutures, X rays, blood and chaos. There was no time to think, only to react and pray that responses—correct responses—were ingrained.

Several times during the frenetic dance from patient to patient, Mac had looked up to see the new nurse close by, ministering to the wounded.

Twice they found themselves working over the same injured victim.

She worked well, he noted. And quickly, as if she'd been in these situations countless times before. He'd known new nurses to buckle under pressure. But then, he remembered, Jorge had said she was a transfer from San Francisco General. That made her somewhat seasoned.

He couldn't help wondering why she'd transferred. She was obviously good at her job, The brittle voice she'd directed at him was nowhere in evidence when she spoke to a terrified woman, who was afraid she was going to lose her leg. Jolene stood, holding the woman's hand as he worked feverishly to stabilize the woman in order to rush her into surgery.

"Okay," Mac announced the moment Wanda told him there was an O.R. free, "she's ready to go up."

Frightened brown eyes shifted toward him. "Am I going to lose it?" the woman cried, hysteria barely contained in her voice.

"Not a chance," he told her, smiling. "You'll be dancing in three months."

His words earned him another cool look from Jolene as she helped push the gurney out into the hall and toward the elevator. Now what had he said?

He had no time to ponder on it. Someone else was calling for him. Stripping off the yellow paper gown, he slipped into the one that Martha Hayes was holding out for him.

"Let's roll," he said to the young nurse.

Eventually, just as Mac's back was beginning to ache in fierce protest—reminding him of the strain he'd received over a dozen years ago on the football field—the chaos receded as abruptly as it had begun.

He glanced over toward the rear doors, holding his breath, unwilling to release his hold on the adrenaline that was keeping him going.

The doors remained closed.

"That's the last of them, Dr. Mac," Wanda told him wearily.

Mac rotated his neck, trying to reduce the tension that had knotted itself there. "Gee, just when we were beginning to have fun," he muttered.

With relief, he shed the last of an endless series of yellow paper gowns he'd hastily put on these last few hours and then glanced at his watch. The balcony collapse had eaten away his time.

So much for a leisurely pace, he thought. If he was particularly quick about it, he had just enough time to go home, shower and change before he had to leave again.

As he turned to throw away the last gown, Jolene passed him on her way to the other end of the E.R. She spared him a look that could have served as the standard for temperatures used in cryogenic refrigeration.

Mac looked at Wanda. "Are there icicles on me?"

Wanda laughed, pouring herself a mug of coffee that had to be thicker than plasma by now. "She doesn't care for doctors."

He watched the way Jolene's trim figure moved as she walked. Somewhere, there had to be a mold in God's supply closet marked Perfect. "So I've heard."

Wanda noted the way he looked after the other woman. She knew that look. It had interest written all over it. "But she's a damn good nurse."

"Looks it," he agreed. He wasn't thinking about the woman tending to his fevered brow. Not in that context, anyway.

Wanda chuckled and shook her head. "You're wasting your time, Dr. Mac. That's one lady who isn't interested in you playing doctor."

He grinned. "Yet," he corrected.

Wanda counted herself among the number who formed Harrison MacKenzie's fan club. Not because of his male appeal or the sexy way he could look at a woman—Wanda had been happily married to the same man now for thirty-two years—but because Dr. Mac was good people. The best. And excellent at what he did. She'd seen him walk that extra mile or so on more than one occasion. For that reason, she didn't want to see his ego bruised.

"Dr. Mac, I wouldn't want to see you fall flat on your—" Tilting her head, her eyes washed over his slim hips and taut posterior. She grinned broadly as she concluded. "Face."

He patted her arm, still watching Jolene as she disappeared behind a curtained area. "Not to worry, Wanda. I have no intentions of doing that."

"To stay on the safe side, I won't watch." Wanda laughed, turning back to her work.

Mac, on the other hand, had never played it safe. Not on this playing field at any rate. He didn't intend to start now.

Chapter Two

Mac had almost missed him.

In a hurry to get back into his civilian attire so he could get home in time for his date, Mac had walked right by the supply closet and almost missed the sound entirely.

It wasn't as if there was no other noise within the area. Even an E.R. at rest still hummed with the regular sounds of human activity.

But this sound was different.

This was whimpering—like a small, wounded animal that was afraid of being found.

Mac stopped, listening for a direction, a source to the sound and abruptly realized that he had walked right by it without knowing it.

Backtracking, he paused before the supply door, listening more closely.

Debating.

If he was wrong, if the sound he heard wasn't the kind caused by fear but instead a little squeal of pleasure escaping, then he would be intruding on territory he himself had traversed more than once. Within each hospital there were little out of the way pockets to which members of the staff occasionally escaped whenever they found themselves being drawn together by feelings that couldn't be put on hold.

He listened intently. No noise. Maybe he'd been mistaken after all.

Mac was all set to chalk the whole thing up to his imagination when the sound came again, this time even more muffled than before. Even more distressed.

Not his imagination, he thought. He just hoped he wasn't about to walk in on something he shouldn't.

Holding his breath, Mac slowly eased the door open and took a quick look inside the unlit, almost airless enclosure.

At first glance, there appeared to be no one there. Only shelves of neatly stacked bed linens and blankets crowding against one another.

And then he saw him. A little boy of no more than about five. If he was six, it was a particularly small six.

The boy was huddled on the floor in the far corner of the closet, his head buried in a towel, the towel firmly pressed against his knees.

Well, that would explain the muffled sound, Mac thought. But not what the boy was doing there in the first place.

Mac glanced again at his watch. Minutes were melting away and so was his safety margin. At this rate, there wasn't going to be time for a shower. Probably the only thing he could manage would be to change his shirt. If he left now.

The debate whether to leave or to linger a few more minutes was over with in less than a heartbeat. There were more important things right now than getting a clean shirt.

"Hey partner," Mac said softly, edging his way into the small area, "trying out our towels to see if they're soft?"

The small, dark head jerked up, then down again, as if the boy had remembered something and pressed his face against the towel again. He said nothing. Mac could have sworn the boy was trying to disappear into the very weave.

Feeling the wall, Mac found the light and flipped it on, then closed the door behind him. He took a couple of more steps toward the boy, approaching him the way he might a frightened, wounded animal he didn't want to scare away.

"Oh, I get it. You're the strong, silent type." Standing in front of him now, Mac crouched down before the boy, who seemed to physically shrink away even further. "You know, you're going to suffocate if you burrow any further into that towel." Mac addressed his words to the top of the boy's dark head. "I'm Dr. Mac. They let me play here sometimes. What's your name?"

There was no response.

Mac took it in stride. Shyness was not something new to him.

"Nameless, huh? Okay, Nameless, I know there's got to be someone looking for you so why don't we blow this Popsicle stand and get out where they've got a better chance of seeing you?''

Still holding the towel to part of his face, the boy raised his head, allowing one dark eye to warily look up at Mac.

There was a bloodstain slowly coming through the corner of the towel closest to the boy's face. The boy was hurt. Had he come in with the balcony victims and had somehow been missed?

Mac didn't think that very likely. The youngest person treated from the party had been a nineteen-year-old. This one didn't look old enough to spell ''balcony,'' much less be on one while a bunch of so-called adults did their best to emulate a frat house prank.

Mac deliberately kept his voice calm, cheery, knowing that anything less would send the boy withdrawing even further into himself. A traumatized patient was just that much harder to deal with.

He thought about his nephew and pretended he was talking to Kirby. His sister's youngest had always been more than a handful.

''Ah, I see an eye. Is there another one on the other side?''

Gently Mac began to coax the towel away from the boy's face. The bandage that was barely resting against the little boy's cheek had been applied by an amateur, very possibly the boy himself, and was about to come off any second. There was blood, both dried and fresh all along the small face.

Whatever had happened, Mac judged, had happened fairly recently.

When he reached for the bandage, the boy pulled back, his eyes wide, frightened. Mac waited a beat.

"C'mon, Nameless, let me see. I'm a better doctor than I look." His eyes met the boy's and his tone softened even more. It was soft, comforting. Questions filled his head, but they could wait for a little while. "I won't hurt you, I promise."

The boy whimpered again in fearful anticipation. He was shaking, Mac realized, but he didn't shrink away this time and allowed himself to be examined.

It wasn't pretty. There was a four-inch jagged laceration running along his left cheek. It had just missed his eye.

Mac felt like someone had stuck a red-hot poker in his stomach.

"You're not part of the people who just came in, are you?" he murmured. It was a rhetorical question. The boy stared at him with wide eyes. "No, I guess not." An urge to hug the boy swept over Mac, but he knew that would only frighten him even more. No sudden moves, no matter how altruistic. "Did someone do this to you?" The boy's silence answered Mac's question for him. Had it been an accident, he was certain that the boy, frightened or not, would have volunteered the information. "Okay, come with me. We're going to make you good as new."

Mac didn't bother adding that the promise couldn't be fulfilled immediately, that it would take some time and more than one operation to make things right, but those were details a frightened little boy didn't need to hear right now. What he needed most was comfort.

He could do that much.

Very gently, he picked the boy up in his arms.

Turning, Mac left the confines of the supply closet and walked out into the corridor.

The first person he saw was Nurse Icicle. It figured. But he didn't have time to look around for someone else, someone he actually worked well with. The boy needed to have this tended to now, before an infection set in. If it hadn't started to already.

Reaching out, Mac caught her by the shoulder before the woman could continue hurrying away to another trauma room.

"Jolene, right?"

She recognized the voice immediately. Shrugging him off, she squeezed out a terse "Nurse DeLuca," between her teeth as she turned around.

And stopped dead.

Her eyes widened as she looked at the frightened little boy in Mac's arms. Her mother's heart twisted a little within her chest. A child in distress always got to her. "What happened to him?"

"Not sure," Mac replied glibly, then looked down at the small being he was holding against him, his voice comforting as he added, "but we're going to undo it, right, Nameless?"

Jolene stared at the world-class Romeo in front of her, torn between her readiness to dislike him and what she saw. "You don't even know his name?"

She looked around to see if there was a worried parent hovering around somewhere close by, but there were only the same players she'd been seeing for more than the last three hours.

No one looked as if they'd lost anything but time and some skin.

He really, really didn't care for her tone or the cool

way she regarded him. As if he'd gotten his degree from the back of a comic book. But now wasn't the time to put her in her place or to even find out just what her problem actually was.

"I know he's bleeding and needs help. Anything else we can look into later." He nodded past the regular rows of beds within the E.R. kept for standard cases and toward the trauma rooms. "Are there any beds available down here?"

Jolene thought for a second. "They just took two more up for surgery a few minutes ago. I think Trauma Room Two is free." The victims had been doubled up by twos and threes, gurneys wheeled into the rooms serving as beds rather than just used for transport.

"Room two it is," he announced cheerfully to the boy who was now wrapped around him like a small gibbon monkey around a tree, holding on for dear life. Looking over the boy's head, Mac lowered his voice. "I'd like your help, Nurse DeLuca—unless of course you have some icebergs you need to create."

Jolene pressed her lips together, stifling the retort that had sprang up in response. "This way." She turned on her crepe heel and quickly led the way to the room that Jorge had only now freshly sanitized.

Once inside, she closed the door behind Mac, then hurried over to the bed as the boy was placed there. He began to whimper again.

Rather than step back the way she fully expected him to, she saw Mac take the boy's hand in his.

"It's going to be all right, Nameless, I promise." Mac carefully made the boy as comfortable as possible. "You know, you're about my nephew's age.

His name is Kirby.'' He kept talking to the boy as if they were old friends, hoping to put him at ease. ''Kind of a funny name for a kid, but I suspect he'll grow into it. What do you think, Nameless? Think he will?''

The boy took a deep breath, then let it slowly out again. His small chest quavered slightly. ''Tommy.''

Breakthrough, Mac thought.

He looked at the boy innocently. ''You think he should be called Tommy?'' Mac pretended to think the choice over. ''Yeah, that's a pretty cool name. Maybe I'll ask him if he wants to change his name to Tommy.''

''No,'' the boy contradicted softly. ''My name.''

Mac maintained a serious expression as he asked, ''You want to change your name to Tommy?''

For the first time, there was a hint of a smile on the small boy's face as he looked up at him. ''No, my name *is* Tommy.''

''Ah.'' Nodding sagely at the revelation, Mac solemnly took the boy's hand in his and shook it. ''Glad to meet you, Tommy.'' He inclined his head toward the boy. ''I've got to admit that Tommy sounds a lot better than Nameless.'' Still smiling, though this time it was purely for the boy's benefit and not easy, Mac looked into the boy's eyes. ''Who did this to you, Tommy?''

She'd been grudgingly giving him points for his behavior toward the boy, but the insensitive, not to mention possibly incorrect nature of the question had Jolene taking offense for the boy's absent parents. ''You can't just assume—''

The woman was really beginning to get on his

nerves. Not even sparing her a glance, Mac held his hand up to silence her. His entire attention was focused on the boy. He needed to bridge this gap that existed between Tommy and the rest of the world.

"You can trust me, Tommy," Mac assured him softly. "I'll make sure it doesn't happen to you again."

A shaky sigh came from the boy's lips and then he pressed them together before raising his eyes to Mac's. His lower lip trembled, as if he was struggling against the urge to cry.

It was clear that he didn't want to say anything, was afraid of saying something, whether because he thought he would be punished, or that something more dire would happen to him. To Mac, it didn't matter. What mattered was that the boy was afraid and that he had been harmed. And that he never should be again.

Tommy seemed to search his face before lowering his eyes again.

"Hugo," the boy said so quietly that for a moment, it seemed to Mac that he'd imagined it. And then Tommy raised his head again, his eyes bright with unshed tears. "Am I gonna look like a monster?"

Finally something he could control in this awful scenario. There was no hesitation in his voice whatsoever. "No, absolutely not, Tommy. You're going to be the same good-looking guy you always were.

"Nurse DeLuca," he uttered Jolene's title deliberately, his smile never wavering for Tommy's benefit, "do you think you can put your disdain for me on hold long enough to bring me a suturing tray?"

Without waiting for her affirmative reply, Mac

went on to enumerate the rest of the supplies he was going to need in order to begin the first phase of Tommy's recovery.

He'd almost had her.

Watching Harrison MacKenzie interacting with the boy, she'd almost been touched by his behavior.

But then when he looked at her, every single warning signal in her body went on the alert. This was the arena she was accustomed to. Being treated like little more than a semiliterate lackey by a doctor.

Jolene stiffened her back automatically.

"Yes, Doctor," was all she said in response as she turned on her heel. She went to retrieve the items he was going to need.

"Good as new," Mac promised Tommy again as Jolene walked out, knowing that a child's retention ability numbered in the seconds when it came to fear.

His sister Carrie had gone on to marry a successful stockbroker and along the way had provided him with two nephews and a niece. Mac had instantly evolved into a doting uncle. The trio had given him a broad learning spectrum from which he'd picked up a great deal more insight into dealing with kids than he'd gotten from either his child psychology courses and even his short rotation in pediatrics.

Tommy wrapped his small fingers around Mac's hand and nodded, his eyes if not trusting, at least a little hopeful.

For now, it was the best Mac could ask for.

Wanda stuck her head in just as he was finishing up his work. She'd observed Jolene entering the room with a suture tray earlier. It was Wanda's custom to stay on top of the new personnel—be they doctors or nurses—when they joined her E.R. team until she was sure that were they were well integrated into the whole.

"Everything okay in here?" she asked cheerfully. And then her milk-chocolate complexion seemed to blanch when she saw the patient. "Tommy?"

Mac stripped off his gloves, tossing them into the trash. He flashed a wide smile at the boy. "You know this trooper?"

"Sure I know him. This is Tommy Edwards." There was an infinite amount of compassion in her eyes as she looked at the boy. "His mother, Jane, was a nurse here. One of my best."

That would explain why the boy had turned up here, Mac thought. He moved away from the boy and closer to Wanda. "Was?"

Wanda lowered her voice. That was a whole other story. "I'll tell you later."

"Mom died," the boy said with the on-target honesty of a child.

Wanda came closer to the bed. She threaded her hand through the boy's silky dark hair. Her heart ached just to look at him. "What happened, Tommy?"

"He sustained a laceration," Mac said simply for the boy's sake, avoiding technical terms that he knew would only frighten him. "He said Hugo did it." Turning his back to the boy so he couldn't hear, Mac took Wanda aside. "That his father?"

Wanda shook her head. It was a sad story all around. "He doesn't have a father, he's got a step-father. His father left before the boy was born. Stepfather's name is Paul Allen.'' She'd heard that the man wasn't happy being saddled with Tommy's welfare now that the boy's mother was dead. Wanda stopped to think. ''I think Jane mentioned a dog named Hugo. A Doberman. Said she didn't like having the dog around, but that Paul was adamant about keeping it.''

The man's exact words had been that he'd sooner get rid of the boy than the dog, but that wasn't something Wanda was about to repeat around Tommy.

She turned around again and looked at Tommy. He looked pale, even against the fresh bandage that was covering his sutures. ''Honey, why didn't you come to me when this happened?''

''Tried,'' he mumbled to the tips of his sneakers as he looked at them. ''Couldn't find you.''

''Well, now you found me,'' Wanda declared. ''And we're going to find your stepdad.'' Even if she had to haul him out of whatever hole he was residing in, Wanda added silently. About to pick up the boy, she looked at Mac. ''Are you through with him, Doctor?''

''For now.'' Turning his head, he lowered his voice, ''He's going to need reconstructive surgery on that once the wound heals.''

Wanda nodded as she pressed her lips together. ''Getting Allen's consent isn't going to be easy. Especially not after I strangle that dog of his with my bare hands.''

''My money's on you, Wanda,'' Mac told her, grinning.

Wanda merely laughed in response. ''C'mon,

Tommy. Let's see if there's any ice cream in the refrigerator for a brave boy.''

She scooped the boy up into her arms, holding him to her ample chest. The boy curled up against her, responding to the maternal warmth he felt emanating from his mother's friend.

His eyes met Mac's over Wanda's shoulder just before he was carried out from the room.

''Bye,'' he said solemnly.

''Not bye,'' Mac corrected him. '' 'So-long.' I'll be seeing you again soon. Sure you don't like being called Nameless better?''

The boy giggled and shook his head slightly. ''I'm sure.''

Mac grinned at him. ''Okay.''

As Wanda stepped out of the room with his patient, Mac peeled off the yellow paper gown he'd put on and turned to toss it into the wastebasket where he'd thrown away his gloves. He could feel the other nurse's eyes all but boring into him.

That woman was a knockout, but she could definitely stand to have an attitude adjustment. Too bad he was too tired to do anything about it right now. ''Something you want to say to me, Nurse DeLuca?''

She couldn't tell if he was being sarcastic or distant. In either case, it didn't matter. She wasn't here to strike up friendships with the doctors. But she was big enough to admit when she was wrong. And she had been, at least as far as this went.

''You were good with that little boy.''

He turned to face her squarely. ''Why, did you expect me to torture him?''

She was already regretting her mellower stance. "No, I just expected you to be a doctor."

Mac stood studying her for a moment, trying to make sense of what she'd just said. He failed.

"Is that some kind of code? Because I was being a doctor. Stethoscope, sutures, Novocain," he went down the line of things he'd used in cleaning out, then stitching the wound. "The works."

"No, I mean you were kind to him." Most of the doctors she'd worked with were interested in doing their job, applying their knowledge, and then moving on. After four years, she'd begun to believe that was the nature of the beast.

Still lost, Mac could only stare at her. "Just what kind of doctors do you know, Nurse DeLuca? Dr. Frankenstein and his crowd?"

He was making fun of her. She might have known. Served her right for entertaining charitable thoughts about him. "Never mind."

"No," he caught her arm as she began to leave the room. "You started this, I'm curious."

Blowing out a breath, Jolene resigned herself to remaining where she was until the doctor heard what he wanted to hear. "I'm accustomed to doctors who treat the wound, not the patient."

He was watching her eyes. She looked directly at him. People who fabricated things looked away. Either she was very, very good, or she was telling the truth.

When you hear hoofbeats, he reminded himself, think horse, not zebra.

He thought zebra.

"So that's why you transferred."

Jolene had learned that being closemouthed was a great deal safer than sharing bits and pieces of yourself. Because bits and pieces could be reconstructed to be used against you, or tossed away carelessly. She wasn't sure which was worse.

But she'd just witnessed him being exceptionally gentle with the boy, the way she would have been had MacKenzie acted like a typical doctor in her mind toward the boy.

So she shrugged and gave him an answer of sorts. "Among other reasons."

She was mellowing, he thought. And he had to admit that he liked it. His initial reaction toward Jolene shuffled forward to take the center stage.

"Maybe you can tell me about those other reasons over coffee later if you're not busy—"

"I am." Just because she was being civil to him didn't mean she wanted to sit at the same table.

She'd answered just a little too quickly for him. "You don't know when later."

"Doesn't matter," she informed him crisply. "I intend to be busy until the next century."

He was about to counter that assessment, but his pager went off.

He tilted the small gray/blue device toward him and recognized the phone number as one he'd dialed only last night. Lynda. Somehow, she'd managed to completely slip his mind.

"Damn, I forgot all about that."

Curious, Jolene looked down at the LCD scene with its numbers that meant nothing to her. The question came without thought. "Forgot about what?"

Mac sighed. He was supposed to have picked the

woman up at her place twenty minutes ago. "My date."

Reaching into his pocket for his cell phone, Mac turned toward Jolene to finish their conversation.

But she was already gone.

Chapter Three

Mac snapped his cell phone shut. It had taken some fancy talking, but he'd gotten himself a reprieve. And then some.

He'd smoothed Lynda's ruffled feathers, mentioned an expensive restaurant that was in the offing and what might happen afterward. She'd quickly forgiven him for the fact that she'd been waiting, getting steadily more annoyed, for the better part of half an hour. Lynda had informed him tersely at the beginning of the conversation that had eventually swung his way that she didn't take kindly to being kept waiting by any man.

But then, she'd conceded at the end, she knew that he wasn't just any man.

She'd already softened considerably when he told her about the collapsing balcony and the people who had fallen along with it. By the time he'd ended the call, Lynda would have been willing to forgive him anything and bear his children straightaway.

Mac smiled to himself, anticipating the evening ahead. He didn't take for granted that he was a man with more lives than a cat and twice as many grace periods.

Lynda had promised to be waiting for him with a cool bottle of wine chilling on the ice and a hot body warming on the bed.

Once more with feeling, Mac thought as he made his way to the staff lounge. This time, nothing was going to stop him from making it out of his lab coat and out of the hospital.

Nothing but the sound of raised voices.

He heard the conversation as he made his way down the corridor.

A gruff voice was strained with impatience as Mac heard the man retort, "Look, I don't need any of your lip, lady. You took care of him, great. Send the insurance company the bill. Wasn't me who told him to stick his face in front of Hugo's muzzle. I can't be watching the kid 24/7, I've got my own life, my own problems to keep me busy. Damn kid's old enough to know better."

Turning the corner, less than fifteen feet shy of the rear electronic doors and freedom, Mac saw a tall, fairly muscular man with a weather-hewn face talking to Wanda. Or more properly, at Wanda. He was obviously giving the head nurse a hard time.

She looked as if she was having trouble hanging onto her temper, Mac noted, which was unusual, given that Wanda was one of the most easygoing people he knew. The man's clothes had the appearance of being hastily donned, and he had one large hand clamped tightly down on Tommy's small wrist.

The man gave Mac the impression that he would think nothing of yanking Tommy up by his arm like a rag doll that had fallen on disfavor.

Not your problem, Mac, just keep walking. Door's ready to open for you.

Mac didn't listen to his own advice.

Instead he stopped in front of Wanda and the boisterous stranger, pausing first to smile down at Tommy. The boy looked up at him with huge, frightened eyes, a beaten puppy looking for a single show of kindness.

"Problem, Wanda?" Mac asked in a deceptively easygoing voice.

The look in Wanda's eyes was nothing short of grateful relief. "This is Tommy's stepfather, Paul Allen." Mac could tell she wanted to say something more, but she only added, "He came here looking for him."

Obviously not in the mood for any further introductions or delays, the other man frowned so deeply, it looked as if the expression went clear down to his bones and was permanently etched there.

"Had a hell of a time finding him," Allen complained. He glared down at the boy tethered to his hand. "Kid keeps running away."

Mac continued to keep his tone friendly, but there was no mistaking his meaning. "In my experience, kids don't run away when they're not unhappy."

The remark earned Mac an annoyed glare. " 'In my experience' " he echoed, "pain in the butt ones do."

The man's eyes narrowed as he scrutinized him. "What are you, the roving shrink around here?"

"No," Mac replied evenly for Tommy's sake, "I'm the doctor who fixed his face."

Tommy's stepfather blew out a short breath. "Yeah, well thanks," he spat the words out as if they cost him, then gave Tommy a short yank to wake him up. "Let's go, kid."

"Just a minute," Mac called after him, then took a couple of quick steps to catch up. "We're not finished yet."

The other man didn't appreciate being detained any longer, especially not over someone he considered an impediment in his life. "Maybe you're not, but I am, Doc. I've got dinner waiting for me and the dog needs to be fed—"

That wasn't all that the dog needed, Mac thought. But he knew that getting into it over the animal wasn't going to accomplish anything. His main concern was the boy's welfare and this was going to need kid gloves. "Your son needs more operations—"

Allen spared a malevolent look in Tommy's direction. As far as he was concerned, the boy had been nothing but trouble from day one. "Oh he does, does he? What kind of operations?"

Mac didn't want to get into any long explanations in front of Tommy. Besides, he had a feeling that most of it would be wasted on the man in front of him. He put it as simply as he could.

Or tried to.

"The scar is going to have to be—"

Allen stopped him right there. He didn't have money to throw away on vanity surgery. "Scars are good for a kid. Builds character. Maybe nobody'll mess with him when they see it.'' And then he laughed harshly as he threw Tommy a disparaging look. ''Kid's a wimp, he needs something—''

Before he could say another word, the man found himself being strong-armed over to the side and pressed against the wall. Taken by surprise, Allen let go of Tommy's wrist.

Mac was holding him put with a strategically placed elbow to his chest.

''Hey, what the hell—?''

Mac kept his voice low, even and almost moderately friendly sounding to the untrained ear. But Wanda and Jorge, who had come out to see what the noise was about, knew better.

''Now listen to me carefully, Mr. Allen. A little boy's self-esteem is a fragile thing. From what I hear, Tommy's already lost his mother and he very nearly lost his face today thanks to your dog. He's terrified of that animal. In my book, that means you owe him a little more consideration than he's been getting. Now he's going to need reconstructive surgery on that cheek once the stitches heal. I want you to bring him by my office for a consultation in two weeks. You can come here, or to the office I have in the building across the street.''

Taking a business card out of his jacket, Mac thrust it into Allen's shirt pocket.

Furious, knowing he was probably outmatched, Allen still fumed. ''And if I don't come—''

Mac had expected the challenge. ''Trust me, Mr. Allen, you don't want me to come looking for you. And in case you're thinking you can take me, you can't. I've got a black belt in Tae Kwon Do.'' He patted Allen's shirt pocket with the card in it. ''Do we understand one another?''

The breath Allen exhaled was hot and pungent. ''I can have you sued—''

Very calmly, Mac turned toward the head nurse. ''Wanda, don't forget to call the animal control department so they can check out Mr. Allen's dog for distemper. And while you're at it, get in touch with social services. They said they wanted to be called if there was possible child abuse and negligence suspected.''

Jerking away, Allen moved over to the side and straightened his shirt. ''All right.''

''All right what?'' Mac asked amiably.

Allen fired each word out as if it was a bullet. ''All right we understand each other.''

The smile on Mac's face was cold as he regarded the other man. ''Good.'' And then he squatted down to Tommy's level and took the boy's hand in his. Mac pressed another card into the boy's palm, closing his fingers over it. ''And you can call me anytime you want to talk—night or day. Got that?''

Tommy solemnly nodded his head. There was a slight glimmer of hope in his eyes. And more than a little affection.

Taking Tommy's hand, the boy's stepfather glared at Mac. ''Can we go now?''

Mac spread his hands wide. ''Never said you couldn't.'' Muttering something angrily under his breath, Allen turned away. ''Two weeks,'' Mac called after him in a voice that sounded as if his greatest concern in the world was what to have for dinner that night.

Wanda pressed her lips together, shaking her head. "Never did know what Jane saw in that man."

Mac had never met the late nurse, but he took a philosophical guess at her reason for marrying a man who was clearly not one of the kinder citizens of the world. "Maybe she saw something in him that we can't."

Wanda could only shrug, resigned to ignorance. "Maybe. You know, if you hadn't come along, I would have decked that man."

"Now *that* I would have paid to see." Mac laughed. "Good night, Wanda," he said cheerfully.

He got exactly two feet farther in his escape when someone called out to him.

"Oh, Dr. Mac, could you—?"

Mac didn't even turn around. Instead he stepped up his pace.

"Nope, no way." He raised his hands as if to ward off anything else that might be coming his way. "I'm out of here. Now."

He hurried out through the rear doors before someone else managed to waylay him. The place, he decided, was harder to shed than a wad of gum stuck in a little girl's hair.

Just on the other side of the doors, Jolene watched him make his way out of the immediate parking area toward the larger one reserved for doctors. She thought of the last comment he'd made to her when his pager went off.

"Well, he certainly is in a hurry to get to his date," she said to Wanda.

One more hour to go, Wanda thought, rounding the main desk and claiming her chair. Not that she got that much opportunity to sit at this job. In her mind's eye, she replayed Mac pushing Tommy's stepfather against the wall. She could have cheered. No doubt about it, Mac was her hero. After the father of her children, of course she added with a mental smile.

She flipped open a chart. "Man deserves to play hard after the day he put in."

From everything Rebecca had said to her, playing hard was never a problem for the good doctor. "Nothing he didn't sign on for by going to medical school," Jolene commented.

Wanda looked up. Dr. Mac didn't need her to defend him, but she felt a need to say something, especially after he had come to Tommy's aid that way. She had a very soft spot in her heart for the boy. "As far as I know, they don't give a course on how to handle self-centered bastards."

Jolene thought of her own ex. And a few physicians she'd had run-ins with along the way. "They should start," she agreed, "by setting up a series of classes in nursing school."

Wanda said nothing, just laughed. These two, she thought, were on a collision course. It was just a matter of time.

And if she was lucky, she was going to have herself a ticket on the fifty-yard line. It was something to look forward to.

Mac frowned.

Ordinarily he could compartmentalize his thoughts and place them out of the way, sequestering them to the far recesses of his mind where they couldn't bother him. It was the foundation for his ability to be able to both work hard and play hard, each of which he found important to maintaining a healthy outlook on life and a good balance in his life.

But even as he found himself in the company of a voluptuous woman whose morals appeared to be as easily shed as a pair of sunglasses, Mac was preoccupied. His thoughts were continually being kidnapped by a small boy with huge eyes and a dropdead gorgeous nurse with an attitude problem.

Several times in the evening, Lynda had to tap him on the shoulder to get his attention.

The evening had ended the way neither one of them would have imagined. He kissed the woman goodnight and left her at her door even after she'd invited him in for a nightcap and whatever else might follow. Twice.

Frustrated, Lynda shouted after him. "I liked you better in the elevator." The pronouncement was followed by a thunderous slamming of her front door that rocked the night air.

He made a mental note to send her flowers and a short apology. She deserved more than half a date.

And he, Mac thought, getting back into his car, deserved to know what it was about Jolene DeLuca that crawled under his skin and remained there, like an unfortunate brush with poison oak.

Mac slipped out of his lab coat and hung it in his locker. A week had gone by without his having run into the feisty San Francisco transplant. Eight days to be exact.

He figured it was just as well. There was no sense, as his mother had once said, in borrowing trouble.

Except that Margaret MacKenzie had been talking about the institution of marriage at the time. She maintained that the state of matrimony was not worth the trouble it generated.

Remembering now, he shook his head. It was one of the few times he ever recalled his parents being in agreement.

More than once, he'd wondered how and why the two of them had ever gotten together in the first place. Granted they'd been a handsome couple back then, still were when they'd finally decided to give the sham they referred to as a marriage a mercy killing. But he had always thought that marriage had to be based on something far more substantial than liking the looks of the face you woke up next to in the morning.

His relationship with either of his parents wasn't such that he could ask one or the other for any insight. The only person in his family he'd ever been close to when he was growing up was Carrie.

The same held now. But even Carrie's happy marriage didn't change his mind about the institution in general. Marriage wasn't for him, not even remotely.

At an early age, Mac had come to the conclusion that there was a reason it bore the label of Institution. Institutions were places meant to restrain you, to keep you away from life in general. Prisons were institutions designed to separate the inmates from the rest of life. Marriage did the same. It imprisoned you, kept you from being happy while it sucked out your very soul, leaving behind an empty, useless shell.

Maudlin thoughts, Mac mused.

He walked down the corridor toward the rear of the hospital. He wasn't prone to maudlin thoughts. In general, he was blessed with an upbeat nature.

Had to be the weather, he decided. After three years of dry, almost droughtlike winters, Southern California was finally experiencing a November that was more typical for the region. It had been monsooning off and on all month. Out of the last thirty days, eighteen had been inclement. And according to the weatherman, it didn't look as if there was a letup in sight.

Certainly not today. Rain had been coming in like a gate crasher each time the rear doors opened all through his shift.

Stopping before the doors, Mac stood for a moment as they opened before him, just watching the sheets of rain coming down. The parking lot closest to the building looked as if it was going to be submerged any minute.

The gutters had to be clogged again, he thought.

The problem with living in an environment that typically saw rain only a few months a year, if that, was that people grew lax about things like sewer systems and gutters.

He'd heard that traffic accidents on the freeways were up, as well. People tended to want to escape the rain and drove with less caution than usual.

"Trying to cool down the rest of the hospital, Dr. Mac?" Jorge asked him.

When Mac looked at him, raising an inquiring brow at his meaning, the man nodded at the black rubber mat beneath his feet.

"You do know you gotta step off that if you want the doors to close again."

Max laughed at the well-intentioned jibe. "Just bracing myself for the run to my car, Jorge."

Jorge peered outside. At the far end of the lot, a car drove by sending a three-foot-high splash flying in their direction.

"Gonna get wet, braced or not," Jorge told him philosophically.

Looking over Jorge's shoulder, Mac saw Jolene hurrying in their direction. Preoccupied, she didn't appear to see him. He'd made inquiries and knew that her shift was over for the evening, as well. Timing couldn't have been better. She was carrying an umbrella in her hand.

"Truer words were never spoken." He raised his voice slightly, getting her attention. "But if I wait for a lovely lady to come by with an umbrella, I won't get wet at all."

Picking up the cue, Jorge turned around and nodded a greeting just as Jolene joined them.

Jolene's glance swept suspiciously from one man to the other. The last time two men had looked at her like that, they'd been hoping to borrow her Organic Chemistry notes in college. "What?"

Despite the rather cool interaction he'd endured earlier, Mac smiled at her. "Going home?"

Her response was guarded. She'd heard about what had happened with Tommy's father the other day, everyone at the hospital had. And she had to admit she'd been impressed. But that still didn't change her opinion about doctors in general and MacKenzie in particular.

"And if I am?"

Mac looked at the tan umbrella she was carrying. It matched her raincoat. "I thought you might want to do the neighborly thing and share your umbrella so I can get to my car without getting soaked."

Though he wanted to watch, Jorge tactfully withdrew. He liked Dr. Mac, but his money was on Nurse DeLuca. As a rule, men didn't like to be seen losing and he could relate to that.

"See you," he said cheerfully, leaving.

"Bye," Jolene murmured, but her attention was on the man who had designs on her umbrella—mainly, she knew, as a means to an end. Today her umbrella, tomorrow her clothes. "Number one, we don't live in the hospital, so we're not neighbors," she pointed out. "And number two, it was raining this morning, how did you keep from getting wet then?"

"I didn't."

His smile was definitely too engaging, too disarming, she thought, annoyed. She had to keep reminding herself that she wasn't easily taken in this way.

With effort, she shrugged disinterestedly. "Guess you'll just have to get wet again."

Mac shifted so that he was in front of her, blocking her way. The wind was coming from the opposite direction and no longer finding its way in through the opened doors. "Aren't you up for a good deed, Nurse Frosty?"

The look she gave him could have frozen a bonfire. "I already gave at the office."

Moving around him, she opened her umbrella and took a step out. She could feel him looking at her with eyes that were soft and soulful. Annoyed with herself, she relented and turned around.

"Oh, all right, c'mon," she bit off. When he was quick to join her, she discovered that there wasn't as much room beneath her oversize umbrella as she'd thought. He was standing much too close. "Where's your car?"

He pointed off into the distance, beyond the security guard's post. "In the other lot."

Jolene sighed. It figured. "Mine's right over here." She indicated a small, red Honda.

Peppy and reliable, he thought, looking at the vehicle. He wondered if the same could be said for its owner.

"Good." He slipped his arm through hers. "Then you can drive me."

Jolene stiffened immediately, shrugging him off. "It's not going to work, you know."

His look was a mixture of raindrops and innocence. "What's not going to work?"

"You trying to charm your way into anything," she informed him. "I've had my shots against people like you."

He was tempted to ask her just what she meant by that, but then let it go. "Everyone should always keep their inoculations up-to-date. But all I'm trying to charm my way into is your car."

Step one, she thought. "Why didn't you bring an umbrella?" she asked again.

He liked looking into her eyes. They were so green, they reminded him of fields of clover. He could easily get lost in them. "Didn't think I was going to need it."

She stared at him incredulously. "It was raining this morning."

When she wrinkled her brow like that, a small vertical line formed just above her eyes. He had the urge to smooth it out with the tip of his finger. He kept his hands at his side. "What can I tell you? I'm an optimistic kind of guy."

They had reached her car. She gave him a disdainful look. "That wouldn't be my word for it."

"Are you always this easy to talk to?"

She hit her security beeper. All four locks popped open. "This is my car, you getting in or not?"

"Since you put it so nicely—" He saw the look she gave him, like she was going to jump in and leave him standing there. "I'm in, I'm in." He laughed as he quickly pulled the door open. Getting in, he put on the seat belt and settled back for the short ride to his own car. "So, what happened in your life after you were voted Miss Congeniality?"

She put her key into the ignition. "I scalped my first doctor."

"Ouch."

"Exactly." Starting the car, she pulled out of the parking spot.

Chapter Four

Jolene brought her vehicle to a sudden halt before Mac's car. If the stop had been any more abrupt, Mac had a feeling his head might have snapped off at the neck.

"I take it you were a race car driver in your former life." Even though she made no reply, he wasn't in a hurry to get out. Her car was shuddering and bucking like a mustang anxious to be let out of the rodeo chute. "You might think about having that vibration checked out."

"Thanks, I'll take it under advisement," she retorted crisply, already regretting her good deed. If there was any kind of traffic on the freeway—and she knew it was too messy for there not to be—she was going to wind up being late.

"Well, thanks for the ride, we've got to do this

again sometime.'' With his fingers wrapped around the handle, he made no effort to open the door.

''Do you mind?'' Exasperated, Jolene nodded toward the door he hadn't opened yet. ''I'm in a hurry.''

Mac cocked his head, curious. ''Hot date?'' What kind of a man warmed Nurse Icicle's toes and melted her resistance? he wondered.

Her eyes narrowed. ''You're not allowed to ask questions like that.''

''Sorry.'' There was nothing left to do but get out, which he did. By the time he turned around and leaned in, he was soaked. ''Thanks again.''

''Don't mention it,'' she snapped, leaning over and pulling the door out of his hand. Once it was shut, she lost no time in driving away.

''Lovely woman,'' Mac murmured under his breath. Fishing out his key, he unlocked his car door.

He'd no sooner gotten in and strapped on the seat belt than his cell phone rang. Trying to extract it from his rear pocket without removing the seat belt was an exercise in futility. As he unbuckled again and reached for the phone, he hoped it wasn't an emergency of some sort. He was looking forward to getting to bed early tonight and catching up on a month's worth of lost sleep.

He placed the phone next to his ear. ''MacKenzie.''

''Dr. Mac?''

The uncertain, childish voice on the other end of the receiver sounded as if it was just an inch away from dissolving into sobs. He took a guess. ''Tommy?''

''Uh-huh.''

Immediately alert, Mac sat up. "What's wrong? Where are you?" Visions of a Doberman foaming at the mouth popped into his head. Was the boy cornered? He'd gotten to a telephone, which meant he had to be relatively safe. For the moment at any rate. He thought of the boy's stepfather. Mac's heart went cold. "You sound like you're upset."

A sniffing noise met his observation. "I'm home, Dr. Mac." The boy lowered his voice so no one else could hear. "My dad says the surgery's gonna cost too much, that I can't have it." There was silence for a moment. "Am I gonna be a freak forever?"

Mac could feel his heart constricting and struggled with the overwhelming desire to punch Allen's face in for playing games with the boy's head. But that wouldn't help Tommy any.

"No, and you're not a freak now. You just have a scar, that's all," he said firmly. "And don't worry about the cost, Tommy. Something can be arranged."

Blair Memorial was first and foremost a nonprofit facility that prided itself on giving back to the community. That was one of the primary reasons Mac had joined the staff in the first place. He could have never been associated with a hospital whose first allegiance was to its board. Mac was confident that he could talk to Blair's chief administration officer and make arrangements for Tommy's surgery.

The boy didn't need this extra weight to carry around with him, he thought angrily. What the hell was wrong with Allen?

"Just tell your stepdad to make sure to bring you in for your appointment and we'll iron out everything then." It irked him to add, "Tell him not to worry about paying," not because he cared about the money, but because he knew that he was saying exactly what Tommy's stepfather wanted to hear. It definitely wasn't his intent to make the man happy, but there was no way around it if Mac wanted to help the boy.

He could almost hear the boy struggling with his thoughts. "My stepdad says people don't do nice things for other people without a reason."

Mac didn't doubt that the dark philosophy was something Allen was trying to force upon the boy. "I've got a reason, Tommy. I want to see you smile. Big-time. That's my fee, Tommy, a great big, wide grin. Think you can muster a big grin for me?"

This time, there was no hesitation. He'd gotten through to the boy. "Uh-huh."

"Okay." Mac didn't believe in putting off unpleasantries. He might as well get this over with now. "Tell you what, let me talk to your dad now."

"Can't," Tommy told him solemnly. "He went out."

"Are you by yourself?" If Tommy was alone, he was going to go over and wait until the boy's stepfather returned—to have him hauled in for child negligence the way he should have last week.

"No, Mrs. Peabody's here. She's the lady down the block," Tommy explained, then added, "My stepdad pays her to watch me when he goes out."

Well, at least the man had some decency, Mac thought. Either that, or, more likely, he was worried about running afoul of the law.

There was no sense in trying to get a hold of him tonight. He had no way of knowing when the man would return home. "Do you know what time your stepdad usually gets home from work?"

The answer was prompt. Tommy had already struck him as an intelligent little boy. "Five."

"Great, tell him I'll be calling him tomorrow after five. We'll working things out about your surgery. I promise."

This time, the small voice on the other end sounded eager and hopeful. "Okay."

Mac spent several more minutes on the phone with the boy, reinforcing that hopefulness. By the time Mac said goodbye, Tommy seemed relatively calm.

Hell of a thing for a little boy to be going through by himself, Mac thought as he flipped the phone shut and tucked it back into his pocket.

"Once more with feeling," he murmured under his breath as he buckled up again.

This time, there were no further interruptions as he started his car. Moving carefully, he pulled his vehicle out of the near-flooded parking lot.

No danger of a drought this year. Now the county was on the alert for mud slides. Mac shook his head. Always something. Still, he wouldn't want to live any other place.

Coming down the steep hill that led from the hospital onto the main road, Mac saw something pulled over to the side. At first, all he could make out were the flashing taillights. Coming closer, he recognized the make as one that was similar to Jolene's.

And then he saw someone getting out. The umbrella that preceded her instantly became fair game for the wind that had picked up. The umbrella was turned inside out and then back again before the driver had a chance to fully emerge out of the vehicle.

Jolene.

Stopping his car beside hers, Mac pressed the button that rolled down his front passenger window and leaned over the seat to look out. "Jolene?"

Under any other conditions, she probably would have simply ignored him, or sent him on his way, opting to wait by the side of the road until someone else came along. After all, it wasn't as if this was a deserted part of town. But the wind had already shown her who was boss by rendering her umbrella useless. She was getting soaked. Besides, she was already late.

Thinking that somewhere along the line, she must have crossed some invisible line she wasn't aware of, offending a deity with a strange sense of humor, Jolene sighed and made her way over to the car. She pushed her wet hair out of her face.

"What?" she snapped.

The woman certainly wasn't friendlier wet than she was dry, Mac thought. He gestured toward the car. "What's wrong?"

"My car decided to take a nap—what does it look like?" Jolene could feel her temper becoming precariously frayed.

He addressed her in terms he'd heard his sister use when any of her kids were particularly acting up. "It looks like someone needs a time-out."

Jolene's eyes widened, and she opened her mouth to utter a retort that bordered on scathing. But then she shut it again. She despised being criticized—especially when she knew the criticism was warranted.

She didn't need anyone to point out that she was being waspish, but she'd had a rough day tacked on top of a rough night. She was close to running on empty.

"You're right. I'm sorry." In her present mood, it cost her to admit this.

Mac cocked his head, as if honing in on a strange surprise. "Wow, did you hear that?"

"Hear what?" All she heard was the howl of the wind as another gust came in, plastering her skirt against her legs.

"I swear that's the sound of frost forming in hell." Mac grinned broadly at her from the confines of his warm vehicle. "Boy, talk about a long reach—"

Her eyes blazed as if someone had set a fire within her. Mac could feel himself getting singed…and intrigued.

She didn't know why she was wasting her time talking to him. "Look, my baby's sick, my car's sick and I think I'm getting sick. I don't need this."

Leaning over as far as he could, Mac twisted the latch on the passenger door and pushed it open. "No, you don't. Get in."

She looked back at her offending vehicle. It had been giving her trouble in one way or another since the day she'd bought it, but she wasn't in a position to buy a new one right now. "I can't just leave my car."

"Nobody's telling you to." He looked at her meaningfully. "You do have enough sense to get in out of the rain, don't you?"

More than anything, she wanted to give this hotshot surgeon a piece of her mind. But since discretion was the better part of valor, she held her tongue. If she was being fair, Jolene figured she had that one coming. But only that one. "Yes."

Mac looked at her expectantly. She wasn't moving. "Well?"

Blowing out a breath, Jolene opened the door farther and got in. And began dripping all over her side of the vehicle.

"Boy, you are wet, aren't you?" Pressing the control panel on his armrest, Mac rolled up the window on her side quickly. He reached behind him and got the towel he'd forgotten to take out of the back seat the last time he'd been to the gym. He offered it to her. "It's really coming down, isn't it?"

Jolene used the towel to rub the water from her hair and then her face. Stopping abruptly, she sniffed the towel and gave him a curious look.

"I used it at the gym." He saw her drop the towel as if it was contaminated. "Don't worry, I just had it draped around my neck when I finished my workout. This doesn't mean our sweat glands are bonding or anything."

Still, she folded the towel, finished, then sighed. "I think I shrank an inch just standing there."

Belated, he turned off the engine. The windows were beginning to fog up, creating an impression that they were sealed off from the rest of the world. He forced his mind back on the topic at hand before he let it drift with that image.

"Do you know what's wrong with your car?"

Yes, she knew what was wrong with it. It was a lemon. It happened even with the most reliable of makes. Just her luck.

"Same thing that's been wrong with it the last three times. The distributor cap malfunctioned."

She didn't look like a woman who would know a distributor cap from a baseball cap. The woman was one surprise after another.

Mac looked at her with renewed respect. "I'm impressed, Nurse DeLuca. All I know how to do is jump-start." The startled, wary look that came into her eyes had him biting his tongue not to laugh. He figured that wouldn't go over very well right now. "A car," he added. "Jump-start a car."

The smile on his lips was nothing short of sensual, she thought, and it was telegraphing strange electrical impulses all through her. God, she really was coming down with Amanda's fever, wasn't she? Jolene squelched the urge to feel her forehead.

"Since you probably don't carry a spare distributor cap in your purse," he began jokingly, although if she'd pulled one out, at this point he wouldn't have been all that surprised, "have you called a tow truck?"

Jolene shook her head. Several drops went flying, one hitting him in the eye. "My battery's dead."

Taking out a handkerchief, Mac dabbed his eye. He gave her the once-over with his good one and commented, "Not from where I'm sitting."

Jolene realized she was clenching her teeth. "My cell phone battery. I forgot to charge it last night." She'd started to, but then Amanda had started crying again and she'd left the charger connected to the cell phone, but unplugged.

"Ah." Nodding his head, he unbuckled his seat belt and leaned forward, digging into his back pocket.

He noticed that Jolene was watching his every move as if she expected him to either jump on her bones, or turn into a vampire—possibly both. "Relax, there's no need to be so tense. I'm just getting my cell phone out."

"I am not tense," she informed him indignantly, even though it was a lie.

The look he gave her fairly shouted, "Yeah, right."

"I've seen ironing boards that were more relaxed," Mac quipped, handing her the cell phone. "Maybe nobody told you yet, but I'm not the enemy, Nurse DeLuca. I'm one of the good guys."

She flipped open his phone. The latest model, it had all the bells and whistles. She wasn't surprised. The man probably used the Internet to check up on his stock portfolio, the way Matt used to. "I like deciding those kind of things for myself."

He had no idea why he was as attracted to her as he was. Looks had never been everything in his book. He needed someone to talk to beneath the trappings, even though he had no desire for a permanent relationship with anyone. This thing he felt had to be something like being fascinated with a train wreck— you just couldn't believe it was happening right before your eyes.

"I could have driven right by you," Mac pointed out.

She'd already come up with a theory about that. "Do you have a date tonight?"

"No." Tonight he just wanted to have an early dinner, answer a few letters, call his nephew to wish him luck on his big test tomorrow and call it a night.

The smile she gave him was smug and nothing

short of triumphant. "That explains why you stopped."

She had a nice smile, even if it was a little smug for his tastes, he thought. It irked him that she was so convinced he was the anti-Christ.

He mustered an innocent look. "Why, are you volunteering to be my date?"

"No!" How the hell had he come to that conclusion?

Mac pinned her with a look that told her he was getting tired of her attitude. "Then other than your paranoia, what are we talking about?"

Properly chastised, at a loss for an answer, Jolene said nothing.

Instead she punched out the numbers on the keypad of the towing service her mechanic favored. She held her breath as the phone on the other end rang several times, praying that all the trucks weren't out on calls. Finally someone came on the line. She kept her eyes averted from Mac as she gave the particulars to the man who answered. The man turned out to be one of the drivers who'd come out to tow her before. He was properly sympathetic and friendly.

Finished, she raised her eyes to Mac and saw that he was looking at her. "What?"

"Nothing, just surprised that you can sound friendly when you're talking to a man—unless Pete's a girl."

"Pete's six-three, has a permanent five-o'clock shadow and weighs over three hundred pounds. He's a man all right. And for your information, I don't male-bash—I doctor-bash. There's a difference." She looked at the phone in her hand. "Can I make another call?"

He gestured to the phone in her hand. "Be my guest. I'm not charging by the call."

She couldn't help the suspicion that entered her eyes. It was a leading line. "What do you charge by?"

"I'm not charging at all," he told her. "I'm returning a favor." When she looked at him quizzically, he added, "You drove me to my car, remember?"

Jolene responded with a half shrug, unconvinced that he wasn't going to extract payment somewhere along the line—or think he could. With dread, she started to dial her mother. She loved her mother but the woman's main hobby was playing 20 Questions.

"You know, I've been watching you," Mac said.

Okay, here it came. Bracing herself, she raised her eyes to his face, "Oh?"

"And you have the makings of a pretty good nurse—"

"The 'makings' of a 'pretty good' nurse?" she echoed. "I'll have you know I love my job and I'm a damn good nurse."

"Okay," he allowed easily, feeling he had absolutely nothing to lose and possibly something to gain, "you're a damn good nurse. So just when did you become a lousy human being?"

Jolene slapped the phone cover shut. He had a hell of a nerve asking her such a question. She had no idea why she even bothered to acknowledge it. Or answer it. The man had no business in her private life.

But the words came before she could think to stop

them. "When I saw my husband, the doctor, who I put through school at no small expense to me, performing a tonsillectomy on his receptionist without benefit of surgical tools. That's when."

It was an old scenario. Mac's father had cheated on his mother with fair regularity. Which was why Mac had found the term "sanctity of marriage" laughable. The way you honored the contract of marriage was by not entering into it.

In Jolene's case, she'd probably driven her husband away with that shrewish tongue of hers. "So your husband cheated on you with the receptionist—"

If only. Had there been one transgression, she would have forgiven Matt. Even two. She'd been that in love with him. But there hadn't been just one or two, there had been myriad incidents once she took the blinders off and took a hard look at the evidence. Matt's idea of marriage was to have someone at home to take care of things while he played doctor with every available female body in town.

"And the baby-sitter and the bookstore clerk and our insurance agent—" She stopped before she really got going. "Pretty nearly half the female population under sixty in San Francisco sums it up rather neatly."

There was hurt in her eyes and he didn't know how to deal with it. He knew how to respond to a child's pain, but a woman's was another matter. So he used humor because it seemed like the best way to cover them both. "Busy man. When did he have time to practice?"

She shot him an annoyed look. "It wasn't funny."

"No," he agreed quietly, "I don't imagine it was. But just because your husband was a lowlife, that doesn't mean that you should try to castrate every man you meet.''

Her eyes met his. She ignored the slight unsettled feeling that rose up. ''Not every man, just the doctors,'' she reminded him.

So she'd said earlier. ''Nice to know you're discerning.'' His eyes indicated the cell phone she still held in her hand. ''You said something about making another call.''

''Right.'' Taking a deep breath, she called her mother's number. The phone was picked up on the second ring. ''Hi, Mom, it's me. I'm going to be a little late.'' She paused, listening. ''All right, a lot late,'' she corrected after her mother had done the same. ''But it can't be helped. My car died.'' She sighed, struggling for her patience. ''Yes, again. No, no, don't cancel your date on my account. I'll be there, I promise. I'm getting a ride. From one of the doctors,'' she replied in response to the question that her mother immediately asked her. ''Yes, Mother, the enemy. You know, sarcasm doesn't become you.'' Jolene deliberately avoided looking in Mac's direction. But even so, she could feel the grin that was on his face. ''I'll be there as soon as I can.'' After flipping the cell phone closed, she handed it back to Mac.

His fingers brushed against hers as he took it. ''Your mother's got a date?''

She dropped her hand into her lap, feeling as if there was a current still dancing through her arm. She wondered if he was wearing something with metal on it and was conducting electricity without her knowing it. She could have sworn she saw lightning flashing a second ago.

"Yes."

With a laugh, he nodded his approval. "Nice to know someone in your family has a social life."

Her eyes narrowed into accusing slits. "My social life isn't any business of yours."

Yet, he thought. "Looks like it isn't any business of yours, either."

That did it. She'd rather put up with the monsoon than the likes of him. Turning away from MacKenzie, she opened the passenger door.

Reacting quickly, Mac caught her arm, pulling her back. "What are you doing?"

Her tone reverted to its former icy state. "Getting out to wait by my car for the tow truck."

She had to be crazy. And he had to be the same for arguing with her. "In case you haven't noticed, it's raining harder than ever."

She tugged hard, but there was no getting free of his grip unless he wanted her to be. She glared at him. "I noticed."

His hold loosened slightly, but not enough for her to be able to pull free. "Why don't we call a truce? You stop trying to slice me up with that tongue of yours and I'll behave."

She sincerely doubted that he even knew the meaning of the word, but given the circumstances, she had no choice. Reluctantly she slipped her free hand into the one he was offering. And prayed that the tow truck driver hadn't been exaggerating when he'd promised that he would be "right there."

"Truce," she muttered.

And they were off to a flying start, Mac thought as he echoed, "Truce."

Chapter Five

Jolene gave serious thought to calling a cab once the tow truck had arrived to take away her wounded car. But she was already running late and the last thing Jolene wanted was for her mother to have to change her plans because of her.

So after she signed the necessary paper for the tow truck driver, she allowed Mac to drive her to her mother's, hating the fact that she was now solidly in his debt.

"Not very talkative, are you?" Mac observed as they got back on the road.

In response, Jolene leaned forward in her seat and turned on the radio. She wanted to fill the air with something other than awkward silence, or worse, awkward conversation.

An amused smile played on Mac's lips. He kept

his eyes on the road as she hunted through the stations for one that was acceptable to her.

"Music lover?"

"Something like that." She actually did love music. It helped ease the tension of uncomfortable moments. And right now, this had the makings of a very long uncomfortable moment.

"I like all kinds of music," he told her. She'd already gone through several oldies' stations, as well as two country western ones without pausing for more than a couple of seconds. "As long as it's not opera."

Irritation had her asking, "What do you have against opera?"

Had he struck a sensitive note? Was she an opera buff? Somehow, he thought not. Mac had a sneaking suspicion that if he said the sky was pitch-black right now, which it was, she would say it was light.

He shrugged absently. "Nothing, just don't care to have people singing at the top of their lungs at me, that's all."

They had that in common, though she wasn't about to tell him. Jolene came to a familiar station. Soft, bluesy music filled the car, elbowing its way into the tension. "How do you feel about jazz?"

He smiled as he recognized the piece. "Jazz is good." He slanted a look in her direction for half a beat, wondering if she'd change the station just to be obstinate. "I like jazz."

She left the station set where it was.

So much for being able to second-guess her, he mused. Easing the car onto the freeway, he worked his way past the knot of cars in the first three lanes and into the carpool lane. Unlike the others, it was relatively uncluttered.

In comparison to the rest of the vehicles in the other lanes, they fairly flew, their progress marked in part by an extra long version of "Cold Duck." It made the time pass if not nicely, at least quickly.

"Make a left right at the next light," Jolene instructed as they got off the freeway.

"She speaks," Mac quipped. "I was beginning to think you'd gone mute."

She felt color creeping up her neck and told herself there was no reason for it. It kept creeping. "Just don't see the point in empty conversation, that's all. There, turn there." She pointed at the light that was about to turn red.

Stepping on the gas, Mac made it through the light with less than half a second to spare. "The point of 'empty conversation' is to fill it intelligently and learn about the other person."

"I know all I want to know about you."

"Yes, she definitely speaks," he said under his breath, though intentionally loud enough for Jolene to hear.

Her mother's house was located on a tree-lined street within the heart of a development that was less than a quarter mile from the freeway.

Zigzagging down small streets, Mac finally came to a stop before the single-story building.

Jolene let out a long breath. They were here. Thank God.

"All right, this is it. Thank you," she said stiffly. To her surprise, as she unbuckled her seat belt, Mac turned off the engine. She looked at him, not allowing her thoughts to go any further. "What are you doing?"

He hit the release on his seat belt. The strap eased back. "Turning off the engine."

Hand on the door handle, Jolene remained where she was. "I know that. Why?"

She really was tense, he thought. It was a completely new experience for him. He'd never had a woman react to him this way before. Just what was it that she expected him to do?

"Relax, I'm not trying to extract payment, I'm coming in with you."

Jolene didn't budge. Neither did the suspicion in her eyes. "Why?"

"Because," Mac told her patiently, "I'm cold and wet and I'd rather wait for you inside the house." The rain had abated only slightly, but it was enough to provide a little visibility that extended beyond three feet. Looking past Jolene's head at the house, he thought he saw someone in one of the windows.

Jolene stared at him. "Wait for me?"

Reaching up, he turned on the overhead light. Beneath the bravado, Jolene looked a little uneasy. "You're going to need a ride home, aren't you?" Mac asked.

She hadn't thought that far ahead. She'd just wanted to get here. And away from him. "My mother can drop me off."

"Your mother's got a date, remember?"

She'd forgotten about that. Terrific, Murphy's Law had made another annoying appearance in her life. But now that she was here, it didn't matter if she had to wait. She could call a cab. "I don't want to put you to any more trouble."

"Very thoughtful of you, but I don't mind."

She blew out a breath, frustrated. All right, what did it matter? She'd tell him the truth. "I'd also rather you didn't know where I lived."

"I'll keep my eyes closed the whole way," he quipped. And then his smile sobered just a little. "Listen, Jolene, if I wanted to know where you lived, I could have easily found out by now. Keeping your address under wraps is not exactly a matter of national security." She was wasting both his time and hers by arguing. "Now stop being ridiculously stubborn and let's get out of the car."

Now he was insulting her? "I'm not being ridiculously stubborn—"

The woman definitely knew how to push his buttons.

His tone was even, but he wasn't sure how long he could maintain that. "Fine, fill in your own adjective, but you are being stubborn." Mac got out on his side and quickly hurried up the driveway to the small house.

Stunned, Jolene watched him for a moment. What did he think he was doing? He had no business knocking on her mother's door, especially without her.

"The man's insane," she muttered. "Hey!" she called after him, but he didn't stop until he reached the shelter of the front door and the roof that jutted protectively out over it. "Hey!"

Exasperated, Jolene got out of the vehicle, slamming the passenger door loudly behind her, and ran up the walk after him.

Mac was already ringing the bell.

"It doesn't work," she informed him, taking out her key.

The front door opened just as she was about to put her key in the lock. Her mother had been watching at the window, Jolene guessed.

A woman that looked like a slightly taller, slightly older version of Jolene stood in the doorway. Curiosity was in her bright-blue eyes as they swept over Mac. It was evident that she liked what she saw.

Relief was still settling in. Erika DeLuca had spent the last hour worrying about her daughter. Grown woman or not, she didn't like Jolene traveling around in this kind of weather. Too many accidents.

But it looked as if, at least from appearances, her daughter had struck gold.

"What are you yelling about, Jo? They could probably hear you clear down the block." Erika's expression brightened as she smiled at Mac. "Hello, I'm Erika DeLuca, Jolene's mother. And you are?"

They were on the cusp of a replay of the Great Deluge and her mother was playing matchmaker. "Wet, Mother," Jolene told her tersely. "He's wet, I'm wet, we're wet. Hold onto the introductions until we get inside."

Erika stepped back, opening the door wider. "Sorry about that." The apology was to Mac.

Walking in, Mac grinned at the older woman. "Snaps your head off, too, does she?"

Erika nodded as she closed the door behind them. The wind was beginning to pick up again, baying mournfully like a lone coyote.

"Oh, all the time. Been that way ever since she

was a little girl.'' Erika took an instant liking to the
man who had brought her daughter to her door. ''I
think it was because I didn't breast-feed her.''

Jolene swung around, horrified at the intimate tidbit
her mother'd just shared as if she were reciting the
latest Dow Jones quote. ''Mother!''

Erika looked unfazed. ''Sorry.'' The word was directed to Mac again, not her daughter. ''I embarrass
her a lot. She has trouble with my being open.''

Why was her mother doing this to her? Had she
forgotten what Matt had been like? What he was undoubtedly still like? Charming to the nth degree. Harrison MacKenzie could have been her ex-husband's
clone.

''I have trouble with you talking to strangers,
Mother,'' she informed her sternly.

Erika looked at her with wide eyes. Mac had a
feeling there was a very sharp lady under that innocent expression. ''He's not a stranger, dear. He drove
you here. You must have talked in the car.''

''Actually,'' Mac interjected, ''she played music.''

Erika nodded. The information didn't surprise her.
''She does that when she's trying to avoid things.''

Given half a chance, her mother would probably
launch into potty training stories next. Well, she
wasn't about to give her that chance. Jolene stepped
in between her mother and Mac, ignoring the fact for
a second that the movement brought her closer to
Mac.

''Mother, don't you have a date to get ready for?''

Erika gave no indication that she was about to retreat anytime soon. Her smile widened as she looked

at Mac. "Yes, but men don't mind being kept waiting if it's worth it."

Turning, she winked at Jolene.

The latter wished she had the ability to disappear at will. That not being a possibility, she turned to the only ammunition she had left with which to distract her mother. "How's Amanda?"

The grandmother and nurse in Erika took center stage. "Still fussing, but her fever's gone, thank goodness. I think the worst of it is over." That said, she turned her attention back to Mac. "So, tell me, do you work with my daughter?"

Mac grinned and glanced toward Jolene before answering. "I try to."

God, she could just see the two of them huddled over in a corner, talking like old friends. Or conspirators. What was her mother thinking? "Mother, don't encourage him."

Erika was nothing if not honest. "Why not? From where I'm standing, he looks worth the trouble."

Mac's eyes danced as he turned them on Jolene. "Why aren't you more like your mother?"

A frustrated, near guttural and totally unintelligible sound escaped Jolene's lips. "If you'll excuse me, I'm going to see my daughter." With that, she strode out of the living room and down the small hall.

Mac extended his hand to the older woman. "Jolene didn't get around to saying it, but I'm Dr. Harrison MacKenzie."

Erika slipped her hand into his. Strong, firm grip. Said a lot about a man, she thought. None of this light, perfunctory stuff. He wasn't afraid to meet a woman halfway. She liked that.

Her eyes became a touch more serious as she dropped her hand to her side. "You'll have to forgive my daughter, she's had a rather tough time of it lately. It's not easy starting over again. And her husband didn't have the decency to die on her, giving her closure."

Mac laughed at the woman's candidness. He'd always liked honesty. It made things less complicated. "I take it you didn't like your son-in-law very much."

"Ex-son-in-law," Erika corrected him happily. "And I would have liked him fine if he had been fried or fricasseed. As it was, he was left unscathed." She shook her head, remembering. She'd had a bad feeling about Matt from the start, but had chalked it up to her reluctance to see her daughter whisked out of her life and moved to another city four hundred miles away. "Pulled the wool right over Jolene's eyes. She worked her fingers to the bone, putting him through medical school."

Erika crossed her arms before her as she looked down the hall for a moment. "Put her whole life on hold for him." She looked back at the man standing next to her. He had nice eyes, she thought. And a killer smile. She wondered if he liked children. "And *he* went on to hold everything he could as long as it looked good in a bra—or out of one."

Jolene stuck her head out of the spare bedroom where Amanda was lying down. "Mother!" She had to get out of here before her mother took out naked baby pictures of her to use as a bargaining chip.

Turning around, Erika tried to look contrite but

failed. "Sorry, it seems that I'm running off at the mouth again."

Jolene crossed to her mother, holding a dozing Amanda in her arms. "Yes, you are. And you're the one who used to tell me not to talk to strangers."

Jolene had been her only child, and Erika had been a little overly protective of her. Which was why she blamed herself for Jolene's marriage. Maybe if she hadn't been so protective, Jolene would have been able to see Matt for what he was instead of what she thought he was.

"You were six at the time," Erika said matter-of-factly. "And besides—" she looked at Mac "—he's not a stranger, he introduced himself to me—which is more than you did."

She wasn't about to get pulled into this. "You already know who I am, Mother."

Erika leaned her head in toward Mac conspiratorially. "The smart mouth she got from her father—God-rest-his-soul."

Enough was enough. "Who are you going out with, Mother?"

"Anthony Palladino." It was a new name to Jolene who looked at her expectantly, waiting for more information. Erika smiled. It was as if their roles had somehow gotten reversed over the years. "I met him when I was skiing up at Big Bear."

Mac looked at the older woman, duly impressed. "You ski?"

"My mother does everything," Jolene replied. Though she worried about her breaking her neck in one of her adventures, there was no mistaking the thread of pride in her voice.

"One of the DeLuca women has to have fun," Erika told Mac. She shook her head, remembering her own life when she was Jolene's age. Except that she'd had a good man to lean on. Jolene deserved nothing less. "And my daughter is a workaholic."

"The bills don't get paid if I don't work, Mother." Besides, she loved being a nurse. Even if it meant interacting with men who thought they were God's gift to the world—and to women. She looked at Mac. "If you still want to take me home—"

Erika's eyes instantly brightened. "He's taking you home?"

Jolene's arms tightened around her daughter, who was stirring. She kissed the top of her head. "My home, Mother, not his."

Erika sighed. "A woman can hope." She walked them to the door and kissed her granddaughter. "Good night, pumpkin." She raised her eyes to Mac. "Nice to have met you, Doctor."

He smiled at her warmly. "My friends call me Mac."

Erika inclined her head as if meeting him all over again. "Mac."

Jolene shifted impatiently. She wanted to get Amanda home and in bed. Besides, the weather looked as if it had let up for a second. Now was a good time to make a run to the car. "Shall we go, Doctor?"

Mac spared a moment to lean toward Erika. He indicated Jolene with his eyes. "We haven't made friends yet."

Erika's smile filtered into her eyes. "It takes time to win her over, but it's worth it."

Embarrassed, Jolene rolled her eyes. Pulling open the door, she pressed Amanda, who was wrapped in a blanket, close to her until they reached his car. She scrambled into the back seat with the little girl. It was awkward slipping Amanda into her car seat from this angle.

The next thing she knew, Mac had opened the other rear door.

"Here, let me help." Not waiting for her to answer, he slipped the rest of the blanket from the little girl and slid her into her car seat. "Hi, honey. I'm Dr. Mac. I'm a friend of your mom's."

"You shouldn't lie to her," Jolene said.

Mac slid the straps expertly into place around the small body. His eyes met hers. "I didn't."

Jolene felt something warm shiver down her spine and told herself it was just due to the shift in temperature between being outside the car and inside it.

Mac withdrew, closing the door. Rounding the rear of the car quickly, Mac got in behind the wheel. He ran his hand through his hair before turning around. Drops rained everywhere.

"Everyone set?"

"Yes." At a temporary loss, Jolene felt she had to say something. "How did you learn how to work children's car seat belts?"

"My sister has kids." He looked at Amanda. "Comfortable?"

The little girl nodded, looking at him with wide, interested eyes. A small smile teased her lips. Usually, she was cranky around this time.

It seemed as if he had charmed both her mother and her daughter. Jolene felt as if she was on the outside, staring in, though she had no intentions of being charmed herself. Charmed was just another term for being blinded and she'd been blinded once before. Still, she felt as if she had to apologize for what he'd just gone through. "I'm sorry about that."

Turning back around, Mac turned the key in the ignition and started the car. "About what?"

"My mother."

He laughed. "No reason to be sorry. I thought she was great." The woman under discussion was standing in the window again. He waved as he pulled out of the driveway. "A lot friendlier than my mother."

Friendly wasn't exactly the word she would have used. "Oh, she's a blast all right."

Signaling, Mac wove his way out of the development. "So you reverted back to your maiden name."

Coming out of nowhere, the question left her momentarily confused. "What?"

"Your mother, she introduced herself as Erika DeLuca." He paused at an intersection, waiting for the light to turn green. A car flew by, its tires sending up an intense spray of water that splashed across his windshield, making visibility impossible. He flipped the wipers up another notch and they slid madly against the glass. "I thought DeLuca was your married name."

"No, it's not. That was Jeffrey." She pressed her lips together, wondering why she was even bothering to answer the question. "I wanted to expunge all trace of Matt out of my life after the divorce." And then she looked at the child in the car seat. Her one ray of sunshine throughout her stormy marriage. "Except for Amanda. She's the only good thing that came out of that farce.''

He was silent for a moment and she thought that he'd mercifully retreated into that state. But then he said, ''You know, I think it's time.''

She stiffened, alert, wary. Telling herself she'd been a fool for trusting him to take her anywhere. ''Time? Time for what?''

''For you to give me your address,'' he replied simply. Slowing down by a curb, he turned around to look at her ''Unless you want me to drive around aimlessly for the next few hours.''

Right, she'd forgotten to give him that. ''I live on Baylor Street.''

That was two developments over, in a place whimsically named Serendipity Park. ''Any particular house on Baylor Street?''

Did he enjoy making her feel like she was mentally deficient? ''It's 1242.''

''Now we're getting someplace.'' He could almost hear her thoughts. ''Don't worry, I won't sell the address to the highest bidder, or put it on a mailing list. I'll just post it in an adult chat room—'' Raising his eyes to the rearview mirror, he saw the apprehensive look in her eyes. The woman needed to do some serious lightening up. ''I'm kidding, Nurse DeLuca.'' He paused for a moment, knowing he had no business asking and that she wouldn't appreciate it. He asked anyway. ''Did he take all the humor out of your life?''

She raised her chin slightly, as if getting ready for an unpleasant confrontation. ''He?''

''Your ex.''

"No." And then, for reasons she didn't fathom and didn't begin to explore, she relented. "Maybe."

Before Mac could ask anything else, Amanda began to whimper and fuss. Looking at her mother, the little girl raised her arms, wanting to be free of her restraints.

"Oh, hush, sweetie," Jolene cooed soothingly. "I can't hold you until we get home, you know that."

There was a world of difference in her voice when she spoke to her daughter. He wondered which tone Jolene had used on her husband. It always took two to make a story. "We're almost there."

Her eyes met his in the rearview mirror. "I know how far it is."

He sighed softly and shook his head. "You know, Nurse DeLuca, things might go a lot easier for you if you put down that chip."

Defensive hackles went up. "What chip?"

"The one you're carrying around on your shoulder. It must weigh a ton."

What had she been thinking, letting down her guard around this man? "I don't have a chip on my shoulder."

"Then you haven't been listening to yourself," he informed her matter-of-factly. "I have and you definitely have a chip, trust me." He pulled up in the driveway of the darkened house. "Okay, we're here."

She was already undoing Amanda's restraints. "I recognize my own house, Doctor."

He turned around in his seat to look at her. "You know, we're off duty now. You can call me Mac."

She refused the invitation, knowing it would lead to other things—or so he probably hoped. She had no desire to be a scalp on his belt or another notch on his bedpost or however he kept track of the women in his life. "That's too personal."

"All right, you can call me Harrison if that makes you happy."

She eased Amanda out of her seat. The little girl threw her arms around her neck and then turned her face toward Mac, bright curiosity in her eyes.

"Why should that make me happy?"

He grinned, his smile just the slightest bit lopsided. "Because I hate being called Harrison."

Well, that worked for her. "Harrison it is." And then, maybe because of the tension that had been dancing through her, or maybe because the situation struck her as ludicrous, Jolene laughed.

The sound was a pleasing one. "She laughs." Dramatically, Mac laid a hand to his chest. "My God, you are human."

"Yeah." She thought of her years with Matt and how much she'd loved him. How much she'd been willing to overlook—until he had cut up her heart. "That was the whole problem." And then she shook off her mood. "But I solved it."

He looked at her with interest, trying to fathom the way her mind worked. "You're not human anymore?"

"Not around people who could hurt me." She looked at him pointedly.

Getting out of the car, Mac came around to her side and opened the door for her. He tried to help her out, but she avoided taking his hand.

"I won't hurt you, Jolene."

She tossed her head. It was raining again and she

huddled Amanda to her. "Damn straight you won't. And do you want to know why?"

"Because I'm a nice guy?"

"No, because I won't let you." With that, she hurried up the steps to her front door.

Mac realized she'd forgotten the car seat. Reaching in, he quickly unhooked it and then hurried after her.

She was still trying to get her keys out. "I think you have the wrong idea about me, Jolene."

"No, I don't." Holding Amanda to her, she unlocked the door with her other hand. She glanced at the seat he was holding. Damn, she'd forgotten about that. "You can put that down right there." She nodded at the front step.

"I'll bring it in for you," he offered.

Pushing the door open with her elbow, still holding Amanda, she turned and took the seat from him. It wasn't easy.

"No," she replied. "You won't. Thanks for the ride." With that, she shut the door on him.

Mac stood looking at the door for a long moment. "You're welcome," he said before he finally turned away.

That is one strange lady, he thought as he walked back to his car.

Chapter Six

Jolene sat in the gazebo in her mother's backyard, watching Amanda play in the sandbox her grandmother had bought for the little girl when they'd moved back down here. The rains that had been plaguing the area all month had taken a temporary holiday, promising to return on Monday.

But for now they had the weekend and her mother had invited them over for Sunday brunch and conversation. Jolene and Amanda ate, her mother talked. It seemed an equitable division of labor agreeable to all.

Until her mother changed topics on her, commenting on Harrison MacKenzie and, armed with the best of intentions, innocently disturbing an area Jolene had been trying to avoid.

Since he'd brought her home that night, there had

been a shift in the way she felt as she navigated her way through each day. It was as if she was constantly on pins and needles, waiting for something to happen. She had no idea what, all she knew was that she didn't like feeling this way.

Nothing was going to happen, she insisted silently, toying with a mug of coffee her mother had whipped up. Not if she kept her defenses up and her head on straight.

Defenses. She supposed it all boiled down to MacKenzie. He was at the bottom of this unsettled feeling she was trying to bury. But just because the man had a few good qualities didn't change the fact that he had the morals of a tomcat. Given half a chance, he would pull rank like any other doctor. Anyway you sliced it, she thought, the man was bad news.

Erika felt she'd been patient long enough, skating around the topic like an Olympic gold medalist, giving her daughter ample opportunity to say something. Instead Jo had said nothing. But then, Jo had always been stubborn, even as a little girl.

It was time for direct questions.

Erika raised her mug nonchalantly, her eyes watching Jolene over the rim. "So, have you gotten together with that nice young doctor since he took you and Amanda home last week?"

"Most doctors aren't nice, Mother."

Erika knew her daughter's philosophy about doctors, even shared it to some extent. It was hard not to, given the years Erika had spent as a nurse. There were those doctors who believed their degree allowed them to sail in, pontificate, then leave the nurses to clean up whatever needed cleaning in their wake. But, unlike Jolene, she didn't believe that all doctors were created smug.

Jolene's mother took a sip of her coffee before saying, "This one was."

"How can you tell? You hardly met him."

Erika smiled. The young doctor had been sexy straight down to his toes. If she was twenty-five years younger, she would have given him a tumble herself. "He has nice eyes."

Jolene put her cup down on the table. "So does Lassie. You don't see me running off with Lassie, do you?"

Erika shrugged. Jolene was being obstinate again, but two could play that game. "Wrong sex, wrong species."

Jolene laughed shortly. "I could say the same about Harrison MacKenzie."

Erika stared at her daughter, trying to follow the conversation. "He's a woman?"

"No." Her mother knew damn well what she was saying. "Wrong species—specifically, a doctor."

"That's not a species."

"No," Jolene agreed, "it's a condition, a condition I want no part of. We've already had a doctor in the family this generation, Mother," Jolene said, lowering her voice so that Amanda didn't hear. The little girl was only two, but she was taking no chances. Jolene figured that it was better to be safe than sorry. Matt might be a rat, but he was rat who was a father and Amanda could make up her own mind about his rodentlike qualities when she was old enough. "And just look how that turned out."

Erika didn't believe in sweeping generalities. "Just because the man you married turned out to be Dr. Strangelove—"

This was her whole point. "Yes, but when I brought him home, you liked him."

"Actually, I didn't."

Jolene looked at her in surprise.

"It was the way he looked at your cousin Shirley—" Erika elaborated.

Her mother had said some choice things when the divorce had gotten underway, but Jolene had no idea that her mother hadn't liked Matt to begin with. "Why didn't you say something to me?"

"Because you would have said I was meddling." Erika knew her daughter inside and out. "The way you're about to now."

Because it was her mother and because there was love involved, Jolene surrendered. Kind of. "There's no winning with you, is there?"

Erika picked up one of the chocolate chip cookies she'd baked earlier. The cookie wasn't much to look at, but it tasted like a chocoholic's idea of heaven.

"Funny, I feel the same way sometimes when I talk to you." With a fond smile she looked at her granddaughter who was busy pouring buckets of sand on her legs. "And just wait until she starts talking in full sentences. One of her first will be 'bug off, Mom.'"

Picking up her mug again, Jolene took another sip of coffee. The foam was beginning to fade. "People don't say 'bug off,' anymore, Mother."

Erika raised one shoulder in a half shrug. "Whatever the modern equivalent of that'll be, I guarantee you she'll say it. And you'll shake your head and wonder whatever possessed you to give up your figure for nine months and become a mother in the first place.'' A fond smile flittered across her lips. ''And then out of the blue, you'll get a messy hug and you'll remember.'' Getting up to go inside and refill her mug, Erika kissed her daughter's head. ''Remember, light of my life, not all doctors were created equal. This one deserves a chance.''

They weren't going to see eye to eye on this. ''He's practically slept with every nurse under forty.''

The news didn't faze Erika, but she sincerely doubted its validity. ''Good, then he's gotten it out of his system and he's ready to settle down and be a good, faithful husband.''

Some men never settled down. Her mother knew that, so why was she pushing MacKenzie's cause? ''Doesn't your plane ever land?''

Erika patted her shoulder. ''Several times, dear. Just long enough to take on new passengers, refuel and fly again.'' She lowered her head down to Jolene's level. ''Come fly with me.''

Jolene shook her head. Her mother was an incorrigible romantic and an optimist to boot. You would have thought she would have known better. ''Thanks, but I'd rather be grounded.''

Erika laughed as she walked into the house, mug in hand. She recalled Jolene as a teenager and how many times grounding had been necessary back then. ''Now there's something I never thought I'd live to hear.''

It had been a busy week. Almost too busy. Mac had volunteered to fill in for a friend laid low by appendicitis. That, plus his own workload and the rotation at the hospital had left him little time for speculating about the petite nurse with the huge green eyes and even bigger attitude.

But he caught his mind wandering to her every so often, when there was a lull.

However, those lulls were precious and few. After threatening Tommy Edward's stepfather with filing a complaint with the police about the dog, he'd finally managed to get the man to come in and talk to him. Nothing short of the man's love for his dog had budged him or convinced him to listen.

Even as he listened, Paul Allen looked as if he didn't believe anything he was being told. The man was the soul of skepticism. He'd learned long ago there was no such thing as a free lunch. Even samples came at a cost.

"Why would you do that for me?" the man had demanded gruffly when Mac finished explaining the paperwork that would have to be filed with the hospital's administrative department in order to cover the cost of the surgery. Mac had promised that the operation would take place despite the fact that there wasn't any insurance coverage. Allen was a self-employed contractor and business had been slow. He'd allowed his individual policy to lapse.

Mac didn't dislike many people, but he disliked this man. Intensely. "I'm not doing it for you, Allen. I'm doing it for Tommy." He looked at the boy and smiled. Tommy looked apprehensive, Mac thought, as if he was afraid that the operation wouldn't be performed. That the plug would be pulled.

Not going to happen, Tommy, Mac promised silently, his eyes conveying the message.

Allen's expression indicated that he was still far from turning into a believer. "Okay, why are you doing it for the kid? He's nothing to you."

Mac saw Tommy cringe at the harsh statement. In response, he motioned Tommy over and let him climb up on his knee.

"You're wrong there. He's one less child who has to suffer because of something that can be corrected. If I have the ability to do that for him, to ease his pain, then I'm going to."

Allen's lip curled in contemptuous disbelief. "For free."

Maybe it was charity the man objected to. Mac had already reviewed the hospital's policy in these cases for him. "You pay what you can."

Allen held up his hands, stopping him. "Whoa, I can't pay anything. I'm still paying off my car. There's no money to spare." His tone indicated that his words were final. There was no room for argument, no room for adjustment.

Terse words rose to Mac's tongue all centered on his opinion of the kind of man who cared more about having four wheels than easing the mental anguish of a child he'd been entrusted with, but he let them go. Being confrontational with Tommy's stepfather wouldn't do Tommy any good.

Even if punching Allen in his perfect nose would have made him feel a hell of a lot better.

He was in dire need of working off the full head of steam he'd worked up, Mac thought. It was getting harder and harder keeping his fists from making contact with Allen's face. Which was why he made tracks for the gym the moment Tommy and his stepfather left.

Blair Memorial maintained a state-of-the-art gym on the premises. It was located in the basement and was outfitted with all the latest equipment. The gym had been a gift from Rudolph Heinman, a former patient who had also served as the training guru for several generations of men and women who ached to be, if not Adonises and Venuses, then at least physically fit. Heinman had been admitted to Blair seven years ago to be treated for cancer. After undergoing an aggressive program, his case went into remission, eventually disappearing totally.

Heinman was so grateful, he gave the hospital a grant for the gym, as well as a new cancer treatment wing and renovating the chapel that was already on the premises. He had been a man who believed in covering all bases.

Trying to maintain his cool, Mac hurried out of his clothes and into the shorts and gray T-shirt he kept there, both of which had seen betters years.

Muttering under his breath, he eschewed the free weights and the treadmill, going straight for the punching bag.

He envisioned Peter Allen's face imprinted on the gun-metal gray bag as he began his workout. His fists flew in four-four time, hitting harder and harder until he was fairly panting from the exertion.

"Anyone I know?"

He didn't appear to hear her and for a moment, Jolene thought of just walking out again. But she'd seen the expression on MacKenzie's face when he'd passed her in the hall upstairs. Something had prompted her to follow him. She'd waited outside the locker room until he'd emerged, telling herself it was none of her business. She'd waited anyway.

"I said—" she raised her voice, coming closer "—anyone I know?"

Surprised, Mac stopped swinging and turned around to look at her.

"What?" His first response was, "No," and then he asked, "What are you doing down here?"

Jolene suddenly felt stupid. He probably thought he'd finally gotten to her and she was following him around like a lovesick puppy. What the hell was she doing here? "It's a free gym."

She was still in her nurse's uniform. "You're not exactly dressed to work out."

The urge to utter a snappy comeback was negated by the fact that there *was* no snappy comeback for this. With no options left, she went with the truth. "I saw the look on your face upstairs. I just wanted to make sure you were all right."

The barest hint of a smile crept over his lips. "I'm touched."

"Don't be. It's my training," she told him. "I'd do the same for any sick animal." She nodded at the bag as he took another swing. "Is that Allen?"

Mac stopped swinging again. "What?"

Go away now, Jo. There's no point in going on with this conversation.

Somehow, her feet didn't hear her brain. "Is that Tommy's stepfather? I heard you talking to him upstairs just before you came here."

Mac looked at her sharply. "Adding spying to your lists of talents?"

Defensiveness, never far away these days, immediately took over. So much for a good deed. "I was walking by...your voice carries." Why was she bothering? She began to turn away. "Never mind—"

"No, wait." Abandoning the punching bag, Mac moved around in front of her, impeding her path. It really was nice of her to come. "I'm sorry, I didn't mean to sound sarcastic. It's just that Tommy's stepfather presses all the wrong buttons for me."

Her eyes held his. "I know all about men who press wrong buttons."

The slight smile slipped into a grin. "Meaning me?"

She raised a shoulder, let it drop, avoiding his eyes. "You didn't press, I anticipated." Pausing a beat, she added, "My mother thinks you're a 'nice young doctor.'" She then chastised herself the moment the words were out of her mouth.

The need to take out his aggression on the punching bag faded. He enjoyed connecting far more than he liked venting. "Your mother's a very smart lady. How did her date go?"

With the kind of social life she'd heard he had, Jolene was surprised that he remembered such a small detail like her mother's date.

"Fine. She's seeing him again." There was a special glow in her mother's eyes that she hadn't remembered seeing for a long, long time, and Jolene was happy for her. It had been a long time since her father had died. Her mother deserved some happiness.

"Good for her."

Try as she might, there was something in Mac-Kenzie's tone that just rubbed her the wrong way. ''Right, you believe everyone should have an active social life.''

Why was her back up again? He hadn't said anything out of the ordinary. ''At least one that doesn't have to be worked over by the M.E.'' He tried again, going for higher, safer ground. ''How's Amanda feeling?''

That made twice he surprised her. ''She's better.''

''Good.'' Mac's eyes swept over her face. She looked a little flushed. Did he have something to do with that? He'd like to think that he did. ''And how's Amanda's mother these days?''

Jolene raised her chin. Time to go. ''Amanda's mother is just fine.''

Mac grinned. ''That's my opinion, too.''

When he looked at her like that, she could feel something happening to her knees. It was as if they'd suddenly lost the ability to lock themselves into place. She urged herself to make an exit before they suddenly didn't function anymore and she embarrassed herself.

Abruptly Jolene turned away from him and began to leave again.

Mac put a hand on her shoulder—or more accurately, laid a gloved hand awkwardly on her shoulder, holding her in place. He laughed when she looked at it. ''These aren't exactly made for delicacy. Since we seem to be enjoying a truce here, why don't we explore it further?''

He was standing too close. Why wasn't she moving away? she upbraided herself. Why was she looking up at that almost square-cut, rugged face and those light-green eyes? Was this what a moth went through just before it had its wings burned off by a flame?

Well, she wasn't a silly little moth, was she?

So why wasn't she leaving?

Jolene's throat felt dry as she asked, "And how would we do that?"

There was that wary look in her eyes again. But there was something more, something that encouraged him to push on.

"That can be accomplished in a number of ways. I thought we might try going out, say—" He wanted to give her enough time, not feel as if he was moving in for the kill. "Tomorrow night?"

Jolene's mind went blank for a beat, and then she rallied, relieved that she actually had an excuse because for the life of her, she didn't think she could have fabricated one on the spot.

"Sorry, I promised to take Amanda to see that new cartoon movie that's out." Since he seemed to be waiting for something further, she gave him the name, not that she expected him to be familiar with it. *"Silly Sandy's Big Adventure."*

To her surprise, the grin only grew wider. Pulling her in. "I've been meaning to see that."

Well, now she'd caught him in a bald-face lie. She laughed shortly. "You?"

He spread his boxing gloved hands wide. "Hey, what can I say? I'm an animation junkie and this movie's produced by that big studio in Ireland."

She stared at him. He couldn't have surprised her more than if he'd suddenly announced that he was a mutant Smurf who'd lost his color and taken growth hormones. "How did you know that?"

He liked the way wonder flowered in her eye. "I told you, I'm an animation junkie." He laughed. "And it also helps to have two nephews and a niece who love cartoons and can be used as protective cover."

Her instant inclination to turn him down lost some of its thunder. Something akin to amusement began to form. "I must say you get A for originality."

"I get A's for other reasons, too." He saw her eyes narrow. "I'm fun. Kids like me, just ask my niece and nephews and their friends."

Maybe she was being a little too harsh on him. After all, he had sounded sincere about Tommy Edwards and there had been no one around to impress.

Still, as Jolene looked at him, she debated with herself, wondering if she was making a mistake. "You're really willing to go see Silly Sandy?"

Mac crossed his heart rather clumsily, given the boxing glove on his hand. "Not only that, but afterward, we can go to the Safari Restaurant."

The name meant nothing to her. She suddenly had an image of men hunting scantily clad women who were weaving their way in and out of plastic foliage arranged to look like a jungle. "What's that?"

"You haven't been there? Then Amanda's in for a treat." He stopped. There was one possible damper. "She's not afraid of animals, is she?"

This time, when Jolene laughed, the sound was filled with abject pleasure. "Amanda? Amanda's not afraid of anything. She's absolutely fearless."

At the age of one, her daughter had leaped off her

first coffee table like a fledgling bird attempting to take its maiden flight out of the nest. She'd gone on to leap off everything in the house, as if determined to somehow take wing.

Mac looked at her. His smile was slow, infectious. Drugging her. "Like her mother."

Jolene realized that she was standing much too close to a sweaty man for her own comfort. She could feel the heat radiating from his body. Or was that just her own body getting hotter?

The word "escape" began to whisper across her mind.

"I'd better be getting back, they're probably looking for me." She began to make good her retreat, then stopped. "If someone's looking for you, shall I tell them where you are, Rocky?"

He glanced back at the punching bag. "No, suddenly I don't feel the need to taking things out on overstuffed, defenseless gray bags anymore. I'm going to hit the showers and be up in a few minutes."

It was on the tip of his tongue to ask her if she wanted to join him in the shower. But he knew if he did, he would probably ruin the tiny bit of miraculous headway that had been made. He could wait.

"What time should I pick you up tomorrow?"

There were butterflies in her stomach, flying in out of the blue and insisting on dive-bombing from all angles. She unconsciously placed her hand over her stomach as if to press them out of existence. They didn't go. "The movie starts at five-thirty—"

His last appointment was at four forty-five, but he could have his receptionist reschedule Mrs. Springfield to the following day. The grandmother of four was a semiregular. She only came in to talk and to get estimates on work she ultimately never had done. She'd been to his office three times in the last year already, each time with photographs of women whom she could only resemble if he'd been given the power to perform miracles instead of surgeries.

But Mrs. Springfield enjoyed talking to him and planning. Mac knew it was good therapy for the woman. It cost her nothing, since it was a free consultation, and him only a little of his time. Mac figured he had it to spare. If his sister Carrie had been able to talk to someone in the months immediately following her accident, she might not have spent all those years lost in the confines of a dark depression.

"Then I'll be at your house at five," he promised, watching her retreat.

"Unless there's an emergency," Jolene interjected at the door.

He grinned, catching the slight hopeful tone, knowing what she was thinking. "Stop crossing your fingers, Nurse DeLuca. There won't be an emergency."

"You never know."

He had that covered. "No, you never do." He was looking at her as he said it. "But just in case, I'll leave someone on call in my place. It's not every day I get to see a Silly Sandy movie in the company of two beautiful women."

He was using empty words again. They needed to have this out in the open. One outing was all that was going to transpire between them. With Amanda acting as a chaperone. "That might work on my mother, but it won't work on me."

He inclined his head. "Duly noted." And then he

looked at her, his smile growing just a tad serious. "That doesn't make you any less beautiful."

Jolene turned on her heel and walked away.

She had absolutely no clue what to say in response, so she said nothing. And she wasn't aware of the smile that had come to her lips.

But he sure was.

Her reflection had flashed back at him in the glass portion of the door just as she passed it, leaving the gym.

Looked like he was finally making some progress. Mac whistled as he walked to the showers.

Chapter Seven

All set.

Smiling to himself, Mac replaced the receiver. Mrs. Springfield had called with a question about tomorrow's appointment. She'd been more than willing to reschedule once he asked the woman personally.

He had his suspicions that the sixty-seven-year-old grandmother had a crush on him. While he didn't like to take unfair advantage of anyone—except for John Gilroy when he was playing poker and only because the anesthesiologist became belligerent when he wasn't winning—he'd used Mrs. Springfield's kindly feelings toward him just this once to get her to agree to the time switch. She was coming in tomorrow just before lunch.

That gave her another half a day to leaf through more fashion magazines and clip more photographs. She always came in with a folder full of them.

Everyone had to have a hobby, Mac thought, hurrying out of the office. His hobby was dating pretty women. The more, the better, because the more, the less chance there was in getting hooked on one and making the kind of mistake his parents had made.

Even Carrie had made one in her first marriage. That his sister had had enough courage to rally and give the whole marriage thing a second try was to her credit. In the long run, Mac figured Carrie was a lot braver than he was.

"Better man than I, Gunga-din," he said under his breath as he walked out of his office.

His receptionist looked up from her computer. "Excuse me?"

"Nothing, Mavis. See you in the morning."

Her goodbye echoed behind him as he hurried out the door and to where his car was parked. Habit had him glancing at his watch as he got in behind the wheel. There wasn't all that much time to spare.

He went straight from the office to Jolene's house, expertly weaving his vehicle in and out of traffic and completing the trip in less than twenty minutes, despite the fact that at this time of evening, the roads were more than a little crowded.

Jolene came to the front door as a third ring pealed through the house. There was a moment there that she'd deliberated grabbing her daughter, escaping through the back door and making her way over an adjoining neighbor's fence.

Instead she looked into the side mirror to make sure her hair was in place.

As if that mattered.

All the man probably cared about was if the vital organs were in place, and maybe not even that.

Sorry, MacKenzie, no rolls in the hay on the agenda tonight, I'm afraid.

Behind her, Amanda was ordering her to "open it, Mamma, open it." The stray thought came to her that Amanda was going to be the kind of child who was going to open gifts in the morning instead of savoring them and opening them at the end of the day.

Taking a deep breath, feeling suddenly very nervous, Jolene opened the door.

He was there, big as life and, if she were being honest with herself, a great deal handsomer.

"Hi."

"Hi," she echoed stiffly, her mouth as dry as if she'd just plowed seven miles of unirrigated desert with it.

Mac waved at Amanda who was shifting excitedly from foot to foot.

"Didn't we have a date tonight?" he asked Jolene. "You look disappointed."

"I didn't think you'd come."

Amusement tugged at his mouth. "And you look disappointed because I did, or because you're wrong?" he wanted to know. "Or did you just receive last month's electricity bill?"

"Never mind," she murmured, thinking it safest not to select an answer from the multiple choice array he'd just given her. Instead she grabbed her purse from the sofa where she'd left it and slung it over her shoulder before bending down to pick up her daughter. "We're going to have to move fast if we don't want to miss the beginning of the movie."

He was right behind her, pulling the door closed. "Moving fast is my specialty."

She shot him a look.

"I just bet it is. We'll use my car," she told him. She'd left it parked in the driveway. "Saves time not switching Amanda's car seat."

"Fair enough." Mac look at the little girl she was holding. Nothing appeared to be wrong. "Why aren't you letting her walk to the car?"

"Because I can still move faster than she does."

Her instincts had told her to leave five minutes ago, before he arrived, and then blame it on a scheduling problem if he asked about it the next day. She should have followed through.

The butterflies in her stomach were taking steroids. Reaching into her pocket, she fumbled for her car key.

"Here, let me have her." The little girl fairly glowed as he reached for her. Mac settled her in the crook of his arm. "Hi, Amanda, remember me?"

In response, Amanda nodded, her golden hair bouncing up and down like delicate clouds playing a game of tag with the wind. Her broad smile seemed to travel from one small ear to the other.

"Uh-huh."

Holding her to him with one hand, Mac pretended to shield his eyes with the other.

"Wow, what a killer smile. It's brighter than the sun." And then he dropped his hand and looked at the little girl he had tucked against him. "Think you can teach your mom how to smile? I think her smile muscles went away from lack of use."

"Mamma smiles," Amanda told him solemnly.

"Ah." His eyes met Jolene's over Amanda's head. "Something to live for."

Jolene unlocked the rear passenger door for Amanda. "I smile when there's something to smile about."

"Then you'll be smiling at the movie," he assumed. She could have sworn there was a twinkle in his eye, but it was probably a trick of the setting sun. "That's okay, I can experience things by proxy." He winked at Amanda, who giggled. "I'll just pretend it's intended for me and not Silly Sandy."

With Amanda safely tucked into her car seat, Mac rounded the rear of the car and went to the front passenger seat.

When he got in, Jolene looked at him in surprise.

"Don't you want to drive?" Not that she would let him, of course, but she thought it unusual that he didn't just automatically come over to the driver's side and hold his hand out for her keys. The men she knew all liked being in control.

He slipped on the seat belt. "Not particularly. It's your car."

Jolene got in behind the wheel. "Most men want to drive."

The look he gave her penetrated through her aqua sweater and went clear through to her spine. She discovered that she was having a little trouble breathing and searched for the button on the armrest's control panel to open the window.

"I'm not like most men, Jolene," Mac reminded her quietly. "Besides, you know where the theater is, I don't."

All very logical. So why wasn't there any air coming through the open window.

Behind her, Amanda began to rock in her seat. "Silly Sandy, Mommy, Silly Sandy."

Mac grinned. "Yes, 'Mommy,' you're wasting time." He tapped his watch. "Silly Sandy is about to start."

She ignored him. It was easier that way than acknowledging what was going on just under the surface. Things she definitely wasn't happy about. "You're absolutely right, Amanda. What was Mommy thinking?" Squaring her shoulders, she put the car in gear and backed out of the driveway.

She couldn't wait to get into a dark movie theater so that she could ignore this man.

The theater at that time of evening was jam-packed and resonating with noise. It was the cartoon feature's opening day and word-of-mouth had spread like wildfire among the under-six set. Everywhere Jolene looked, there were handfuls of harried adults attempting to keep track of gaggles of children.

Holding Amanda firmly by the hand and ushering Jolene in before him, Mac remarked, "Looks like we're the only ones who aren't outnumbered."

She turned to look at him. Big mistake. If she'd been any closer to him, there wouldn't have been enough room to slip a dime in between them.

She suddenly had firsthand knowledge of what the term "steal your breath away" meant.

Still, she managed to force out the question, "Outnumbered?"

He nodded, urging her on. "There's two of us to

one of her. From the looks of it, there's just one adult for every five or six short people.''

Outnumbered was the term for it. And children had nothing to do with the feeling. She felt outnumbered just being this close to him.

Maybe this was not such a good idea. She'd thought that confronted with a kiddie movie, he'd run for the hills, not embrace the idea. If she hadn't gone through what she had and he wasn't what he was, he would have been looking pretty good to her by now.

But she had gone through hell with her husband and MacKenzie was Blair Memorial's most desired hunk—and he knew it. Under no circumstances could she allow herself to forget that. Because if she did, if through some freakish act of nature, she temporarily lost her mind and allowed her guard to go down long enough to fall under this drop-dead gorgeous man's spell, it would be all over for her.

The fall wouldn't just hurt her this time, it would probably kill her.

The trick here, Jolene reminded herself, was not to go up on that high beam to begin with. That meant keeping both feet firmly planted on the ground.

Putting on a pair of blinders wouldn't exactly hurt, either.

Once inside the movie theater lobby, the crowd began to disperse a little. One wall was lined with arcade games that instantly attracted an array of children.

Mac looked down at Amanda. ''C'mon, princess, let's go see ourselves a dog.''

Amanda, in Jolene's estimation, looked prepared to follow him to the ends of the earth.

He turned and peered at Jolene over his shoulder. "Coming, 'Mommy?'"

Her eyes narrowed. There was something irksome about his referring to her that way. And far too familiar. "Don't call me that, Harrison."

Making his way past a mother with triplets, all of whom were trying to outyell each other, Mac nodded. "I think I can foresee a fair exchange in the making, Nurse DeLuca."

Why was it when he called her that, she felt as if he was teasing her? As if he found what she did amusing in some way?

Just her insecurity raising its ugly head, Jolene told herself. Matt had always found ways to undermine her, to make her feel that she was something only a little more capable than an orderly, and maybe just a shade more intelligent than a doorstop.

Mac saw the lines forming at the candy counter. Three teenagers in less than attractive brown uniforms were trying to fill the orders coming their way.

"Popcorn?" he asked Jolene.

She had a tendency to pig-out on popcorn. Another personal thing she didn't want him to know about her. "We're having dinner, remember?"

His smile was getting to be more and more disarming. There had to be somewhere she could go to get shots against it. And him.

"How can I forget? I've been looking forward to it all day."

He hadn't been at the hospital at the same time she was on duty. At least, she hadn't run into him. Part of her had taken that to mean that perhaps he'd thought better of their so-called date and had chosen to face the matter in typical male fashion: by avoiding her. Even though he was here now, she sincerely doubted that he had spent his day looking forward to this.

"Still," he looked at the shorter of his two dates, "What's a movie without popcorn, if only to leave behind?" He temporarily cut Jolene out of the conversation, centering the universe around Amanda. "How about it, Amanda? Want some popcorn?"

The little girl nodded her head vigorously. Jolene had the impression that her daughter would have agreed to almost anything Mac suggested. The man's charm was deadly, leaving no one from two to two hundred safe.

"How about you?" His eyes shifted to her.

"I'll pass." Jolene inclined her head, lowering her voice so that only he could hear her. "You know, you don't have to be nice to Amanda to get to me."

Her breath was warm against his neck, sending a shiver down his spine. Mac felt his gut tighten. Drawing his head back, he grinned at her.

"And here I thought you were leaning over to nibble on my ear." His eyes grew serious, his voice as low as hers. "I'm being nice to Amanda because I like Amanda. I like all kids. They're what we all were before the world hit us with its garbage."

He definitely unnerved her when he looked at her like that. Jolene changed the subject, nodded toward the counter. "There's too large a line. We'll be late getting into the movie."

Mac didn't answer her. Instead he made eye contact with a woman at the far end of the counter who was clearly in charge. Brightening visibly, the woman looked at him quizzically. Mac motioned her to the side and met her there.

He picked Amanda up into his arms. "My little friend here would like some popcorn, but we're afraid we might miss the movie."

"No problem." The words were directed at him rather than the child they involved. The woman seemed only too happy to take this small obstacle out of Mac's life. "Small, medium, large?"

"Large. We're going to teach her about sharing today. No butter," he added as the woman took a large container and plunged it into the sea of popcorn. "We don't want her to pick up any bad habits this early."

The woman nodded. "Very smart." Jolene had the feeling the woman would have made the same pronouncement had MacKenzie said he was thinking of hang gliding off the theater complex roof.

"Five-ninety, right?" Mac handed the woman the proper change. She just closed her fingers over the amount without checking.

"I don't believe it," Jolene declared as they walked away from the counter. The woman went back to tallying containers and ignoring the people lining up along the counter.

Stopping before theater number three, Mac looked at her innocently. "Don't believe what?"

"You just flirted with another woman while you were on a—a—" She couldn't bring herself to call it a date. "On an excursion with me."

An excursion, so that's what she called it. His mouth curved with amusement. "That's not flirting, Jolene, that's just interacting." Holding Amanda's hand, he momentarily set the large tub of popcorn down on the floor. "This—" he slowly ran his thumb along Jolene's lower lip as he looked into her eyes "—is flirting."

She's been around the block more than once, in a souped-up car at that. She'd been married, divorced and experienced all the shades that existed in between the two states. Why then did the entire area suddenly go dark for the space of an eternal moment, as if they'd been thrown bodily into the eye of an electrical power grid failure? And why did her heart suddenly begin beating like a world renowned drummer wired with espresso coffee and a pound of dark chocolate?

She had no answer. None that she wanted to even mildly consider.

"Oh," was all she managed. The lights slowly seeped back into existence and her bearing returned, slightly tilted but there. "The movie." Somewhat shaky, Jolene pointed at the opened theater door behind him. The music had stopped playing, a sure sign that coming attractions were about to begin.

"Right, the movie."

Mac turned toward the theater, his body locked in slow motion. For a moment there, something had happened, had sparked within him, and he'd be dammed if he understood what.

Had to be because the woman was resisting him so much. The last time he'd met up with resistance outside of a high school physics experiment, he'd found himself just entering puberty. And Sheila Royce hadn't resisted for long. She'd kissed him under the bleachers at halftime less than a day after she'd played hard-to-get.

This woman was doing a much better job than Sheila Royce at getting under his skin.

"We'd better get inside," he added needlessly, then turned to lead the way.

Walking in, Mac stood for a moment in the darkening theater, getting his eyes accustomed to the dim lighting, attempting to make shapes out. Or not make them out as the case was. He was trying to scout out three unoccupied seats that were together.

Jolene beat him to it. It was amazing what weakening knees made you do. "There." She pointed to the area for emphasis.

He was still trying to focus. "Where? I don't see any empty seats."

Shaking her head, she took his arm and led the way up to the front of the theater. Part of her was convinced that he'd feigned not being able to see the seats for this exact reason.

The seats were three rows from the screen.

"Too close?" she asked.

He was surprised that she bothered asking him his preference. But as a doting uncle, he'd sat even closer than this.

"No, this is perfect for Amanda." He looked down for a confirmation from the little girl and got it. "No big heads in the way, right, princess?"

She nodded her head vigorously, her wispy curls bouncing again. "Right."

Mac led the way into the row. To Jolene's surprise, he looked perfectly content to have Amanda planted between them. Settling in, he held the popcorn container where it was easily accessible to the little girl.

* * *

It was a ninety-three minute movie…ninety-three minutes of nonstop color, antics and song.

Jolene'd spent most of those ninety-three minutes watching MacKenzie rather than her daughter or the movie. Convinced that this too-good-to-be-true act of MacKenzie's was just that, a ruse to get her into bed, she felt sure that once the lights were down and the movie was rolling, he'd begin to fidget restlessly. At the very least, she felt confident that he wouldn't bother watching the movie.

She hadn't expected him to watch the cartoon feature in its entirety, and certainly didn't expect him to laugh. But he did both, leaning over occasionally to explain something to Amanda. Amanda was eating it up.

Just like a little girl who missed male influence in her life. Who missed having a father.

Somewhere after the third song, a duet sung by Silly Sandy and a purple cricket named Oscar, Jolene felt as if she'd intruded on an exclusive club.

Watching MacKenzie and her daughter, she suddenly felt a lump rising in her throat. If Matt hadn't been such a bastard with an overeager sex drive, this could have been his. Amanda could have been giggling with him over the duet instead of with a stranger.

No, that wasn't entirely right. Even if Matt had kept his zipper in its closed position and they'd remained a family, nothing in the world would have convinced him to go to the movies and spend an evening watching a cartoon dog spread cheer and sing. Matt just wasn't good with children. She'd known that when she married him. She'd hoped, of course, that when their own came along, he'd change. And he had.

Except that the change had been for the worse. He'd reverted back to his premarried state with a vengeance.

"What's the matter?"

MacKenzie'd whispered the question in her ear, his breath caressing her skin, causing a minor warm front to move in over her entire body. Startled, she jumped and looked at him. "What?"

"You look like you're a million miles away."

Amanda looked up at the two adults talking over her head and uttered an impatient, "Shhhh," the way her mother had countless times to her when she was being too noisy.

Mac almost laughed out loud.

"Sorry," he whispered to Amanda. "It won't happen again." To seal the deal, he crossed his heart and faced forward.

Jolene hadn't realized just how appealing his profile was, especially in such low lighting. Or how heart softening.

With effort, she tried to pick up the thread of the story and stop noticing the sexy doctor less than two feet away from her.

She didn't have much luck.

Chapter Eight

The Safari Restaurant, nestled in the heart of the sprawling Bedford Mall, was an experience for the senses that was discernible long before Jolene walked into it. Built without two of its walls, it relied on scenery such as palms, strategically placed fish tanks and configurations of mechanical beasts to lend structure to the enclosed place.

Amanda's head seemed to spin like a top as the food server, dressed as an African safari guide, led them to their table. Jolene saw MacKenzie slip the young woman a twenty. In exchange for that, they were taken to a table that was in the very center of the restaurant. From there, they could see and hear everything.

The food server recited the specials of the day, complete with all the appropriate, cute names and waited to see if anything proved tempting. Mac ordered something called a Rhino Burger, suggesting that Amanda might enjoy a dish called Gibbon Food, which turned out to be home-styled potatoes and grilled, finger-size hot dogs.

Jolene went with the Mogambo Salad and was surprised when the women returned with a plate that took up half the tray and had everything on it but the proverbial kitchen sink. Given all the camouflaging lettuce, the latter could very well have been on the plate.

Jolene felt daunted before she even began. However, Amanda dived in as if she'd been starving for the last week instead of someone who had just consumed more than her share of popcorn at the movies.

Jolene had glimpsed the prices on the menu, which were longer than the names on the items. This was not an inexpensive date. In light of that, since he wasn't about to get anything else for his investment, she supposed she at least should make an attempt at some kind of conversation.

Raising her voice to be heard above the din, Jolene asked, "How did you find this place?"

Watching Amanda's reaction to the different animals tickled him. Mac raised his eyes to Jolene's. "I didn't. Karla and Ethan did."

She wasn't sure if she was supposed to know them, or if she'd even heard him correctly. A person could go deaf working here, she thought. "And they are?"

"My niece and nephew. They're ten and eight." He took out his wallet and found the photograph that had all three in it. He passed it over to Jolene. "But Kirby's the one who really loves this place. He's five.'' He glanced at Amanda. ''I wasn't too sure about a two-year-old, though.''

Jolene handed his wallet back to him. A man who carried around a photograph of his niece and nephews couldn't be all bad, she thought, no matter how hard she struggled to keep the label affixed to him. ''They're very sweet.''

''Yes, they are,'' he agreed with pride, returning his wallet to his back pocket.

He needn't have worried about Amanda's reaction to the place. The little girl looked as if she'd finally found her rightful home.

Very simply, the restaurant was built on the principle of perpetual noise and perpetual motion. Decorated to look like a tropical rain forest, it saw no embarrassing contradiction in having a full-size mechanical ape and a tiger, complete with cubs, periodically letting loose with their respective roars.

It was the perfect place to come in order to entertain a child and not talk to your date, Jolene thought. Not that MacKenzie was actually her date.

He was just the man she was allowing to pay for everything.

The irony of the situation hit her.

All right, so she had joined the fold. She was one of ''Hunky Harrison's'' dates. But only by the most technical stretch of the word's definition. They'd gone out together, shared a noisy movie and a noisier meal, but they were not going to be sharing anything else. Not if she had anything to say about it. She wasn't even going to shake his hand at the door if she could help it.

''What's wrong?''

Glancing up, she realized that he was saying something to her, but only because she saw that his lips were moving and he was looking at her with those piercing green eyes of his. His voice was completely drowned out by the sounds of a sudden thunder shower that was taking place not three feet behind her. The screech of a monkey heading for high ground was added in, making anything short of lip reading impossible.

Mac waited for the cycle to end and the volume around him to lower to a manageable roar.

"What's wrong?" he repeated, raising his voice and leaning toward her. "You looked pained." He indicated the salad in front of her. "Something wrong with your meal?"

She shook her head and regretted the motion immediately. There were seven little men with large pickaxes working over her temple. "I think I'm getting a headache."

Mac laughed. That had been Carrie's complaint when she'd come with them the last time.

"This place'll do that to you." He looked around, watching an incredibly lifelike monkey climb hand over hand between three vines, then return again to the beginning. "I think they've got it engineered that way so that they get a faster turnover with their customers. If you're over twelve, you can only stand this place for so long before it gets to you and you feel as if native drums are beating in your chest."

Maybe that was it. Maybe she was feeling the native drums beating in her chest. She was certainly feeling something unusual, sitting across from MacKenzie like this. She couldn't hear him half the time, but she could see him. See him interacting with her daughter, who seemed to have no trouble hearing him and gleefully laughing at nearly everything he said.

There was no doubt about it, the man knew how to exude charm just by breathing.

But there was more to him than that, she had to grudgingly admit. She'd seen him with that poor excuse for a human being, Tommy's stepfather, the other day. MacKenzie was a man who knew how to get his point across, how to champion an unpopular cause.

Damn, she was beginning to think like someone in his fan club, not like a woman who should know better. A woman who knew that charming men were predominantly all facade, like the make-believe fronts that were made out of cardboard and used in movies. If you looked at them from the side, there was nothing there.

Of course, when you looked at MacKenzie from the side, there was a lot there, a small voice inside her whispered. There was a chiseled profile, biceps that looked as if they wanted to bulge out of the sleeves of the shirt he'd rolled up. A chest that looked harder than granite…

Stop that! she ordered herself.

Because he didn't want to shout and add to her headache, Mac leaned over the table and asked, "In the mood for anything else?"

Yes.

Her own silent response left Jolene feeling more than a little shell-shocked because of what had motivated it. Damn it, for a minute she was beginning to let her mind wander, picturing him as Tarzan, wearing nothing more than a loincloth. A small one. And she was Jane. Waiting in their tree house.

Jolene ran her tongue over her lips before asking, "What?"

Mac leaned in even closer. "You haven't really touched your salad, I thought maybe you wanted something else."

It was an innocent enough statement, why was her mind coming up with loaded interpretations? Because she didn't trust this man, she told herself, no further than she could throw him.

"Popcorn," was all she said in her defense.

Though she'd been adamant about her resolve not to have any in the theater, Jolene would have been the first one to admit that she had a weakness for it. By the time the movie was over, she'd eaten more than half the container herself. But that was MacKenzie's fault. He had kept the tub right within her reach the entire ninety-three minutes.

Interpreting her single-word explanation, Mac accepted the blame gracefully. "Sorry about that. I should have bought a small."

She wasn't about to let him be gallant about this. That would have made him noble somehow and she needed him as tarnished as she could manage. "No, I should have resisted it."

He looked at her for a long moment. "Sometimes, you just can't resist, no matter how good you think your willpower is. It's a fact of life. Everyone's got some kind of weakness." His eyes teased hers, or maybe it was just the lighting. In either case, the butterflies made a return appearance in her stomach.

They were right at home, given the atmosphere. "I guess popcorn's yours."

She was having trouble breathing. There were decidedly too many people in the small area. Too many people, too many things and too much of him.

"I guess."

The smile in his eyes filtered down to his lips. She felt isolated, yet definitely not alone. "Any other weaknesses I should know about?"

With effort, Jolene rallied.

The look that came into her eyes told him to back away, reminding him that he dearly loved a challenge. "I like punctuality and people who know to leave when the party's over."

Jolene found the smile that teased his lips particularly unnerving. And for some reason, the noise around them seemed to reinforce his words rather than drown them out.

"I always do, Nurse DeLuca, I always do."

The hell he did, or else he would have left them at the movies. Right after he'd made the entire theater fade away.

But what was important to her now was that he know that there was no way in hell he was coming into her house tonight—or any other night.

"I guess then," she said evenly, picking at the salad, "that it's a matter of agreeing on the definition of just when the party's over."

"I guess so."

It wasn't until that moment that she realized he'd reached across the small table and had his hand over hers. Alarms went off in her head and she pulled her hand away as if she'd just been burned.

Surprised, Amanda looked at her. "Got an ow-ey, Mommy?"

"No, baby." Jolene looked at the man across from her defiantly as she said it.

And she didn't intend to get one, either.

"Don't wanna go to bed," Amanda protested as Jolene brought their car to a halt in the driveway right next to Mac's vehicle.

She knew this was going to happen. Bedtime was never an easy matter under normal circumstances and these were anything but normal. "It's getting late, Amanda."

With the inborn instincts of every child who had played one parent against another, Amanda looked toward Mac to rescue her. She strained in her car seat, trying to lean forward.

"P'ease, Man."

"Man" was as close as Amanda could manage any part of MacKenzie, or even Mac. He got a big kick out of hearing her call him that.

"I'm afraid you've gotta listen to your mom, Amanda." Jolene slanted him a look he couldn't read, but he could hazard a guess. The woman was waiting for him to say something to contradict what he'd just said. "Tell you what, would you go to bed if I read you a story?"

Amanda clapped her hands together, her eyes bright in anticipation. "Stow-ee."

Leaning back, Mac ruffled Amanda's hair affectionately. "I guess that settles it."

"No, it doesn't," Jolene said firmly. Unbuckling

her seat belt, she turned to look at him. "Reading a story means that you'd have to come in."

"Unless you want me to sit outside her window and do it."

She hated being patronized. "Her room's on the second floor. You'd have to sit in a tree."

Mac assumed she meant the large oak on the side of the house, and he pretended to crane his neck and look at it. "Hard, but not impossible."

Amanda clapped her hands again, bringing their attention back to what was ultimately important here. "Man weed stow-ee."

Mac shook his head, looking at Jolene. "How can you resist this face?"

Talk about an ego. Jolene narrowed her eyes. "I can resist your face just fine."

His face was the picture of innocence. How could someone so guilty look like that, she wanted to know. "I meant Amanda's."

Embarrassed, Jolene could feel color creeping up her neck and face. She didn't want to continue arguing. "All right, you can come in and read her a story. But just one."

The warning was issued to both Mac and his cheering section.

A symphony of boundless energy, the instant she was taken out of her car seat Amanda grabbed Mac's hand and dragged him to the front door, moving well ahead of her mother. It was obvious that Amanda was taking no chances that she would change her mind.

Mac said nothing, maintaining his innocent facade and smiling at Jolene as she unlocked her door.

One story, just one story, Jolene consoled herself.

She'd give him a short one and then he'd be on his way. Maybe one of Dr. Seuss's stories. Still fighting for composure, she tossed her purse onto the sofa.

Mac looked around. It was a small, cozy house from the looks of it, made somewhat crammed by the stacks of opened and unopened boxes that were lining the opposite walls of the living room.

"I like what you've done with the place." He watched her, his eyes dancing. "What do you call this kind of decor?"

"I call it not-finished-unpacking, wise guy," she informed him tersely, closing the door behind her.

This was a mistake, letting him come in here, she thought. And it was feeling like more and more of one every moment.

She extracted the little girl's hand from Mac-Kenzie's. It took a little more doing than she'd thought. Amanda seemed determined to hang on to her prize.

Jolene wrapped her own hand around her daughter's. "Let's get you ready for bed, young lady."

"My sentiments exactly," Mac agreed.

The only problem was, he was looking at her when he said it.

Mac laughed out loud as he watched the storm clouds quickly gather in her eyes. His smile softened into one that could have melted an iceberg at twenty paces.

"Sorry, I just couldn't resist, seeing as what you think of me."

"You—" she raised her chin pugnaciously "—don't know the half of what I think of you."

No, he had a hunch he didn't. But he also had a

hunch he could turn her around quickly enough, given the chance. He took a step toward Jolene, his smile inviting, his meaning clear.

"Maybe you can tell me after the story."

The hell she was. "All I'm going to tell you after the story is goodbye," she promised.

He wasn't about to make his case, not in front of the little girl. So instead Mac shrugged casually. "Whatever works for you."

That proved it, she thought. He was in it for the conquest, nothing more. She squared her shoulders. As Jolene DeLuca, she meant nothing to him. She was just another warm body he meant to climb on and then over. He undoubtedly thought of them as two ships passing in the night, nothing more.

Except that this ship wasn't about to have her bottom scraped by him. She was going to stay in port and nothing he could do was going to make her put out to sea. She'd been there. The trip wasn't worth it.

Closing her hand more tightly around her daughter's, Jolene went up the stairs.

Amanda looked over her shoulder. "Man." It wasn't a question, it was a summons.

"Don't worry, I'll be up as soon as your mother gets you ready for bed," he promised. "Be sure you pick out a good story."

Though she had no idea why, Jolene looked back down the stairs herself. She saw MacKenzie looking at the books she'd managed to unpack and put on the bookshelves that buffered the fireplace.

"Don't touch anything," she warned.

His hand on the spine of a book of poetry, he offered her an engaging smile. "Don't worry, I get sanitized at the hospital daily."

Rolling her eyes, Jolene took her daughter the rest of the way up the stairs and to her room.

The man was leaving the moment he uttered the last word in the story he was going to read to Amanda—and not an instant later.

Jolene waited for MacKenzie in the hallway, watching impatiently as he eased his way out of Amanda's room, then slowly closed the door.

It had taken not one but three stories before the little girl had finally fallen asleep. Each time one ended, Amanda would beg for another, insisting she wasn't "sweepy." Mac had good-naturedly gone from one book to another, reading the parts as if he was giving a command performance before the Queen rather than reading to a bossy two-year-old.

Shoving her hands into the back pocket of her jeans, Jolene fell into step beside Mac. Though she wasn't happy about it, she supposed she had to give credit where credit was due.

"I didn't expect you to make it through one story, much less three," she admitted as she led the way down the stairs.

Reading out loud was something he'd picked up when Carrie's children were still in the diaper stage. It soothed him after a long day to drop by and read to his niece and then his nephews.

He shrugged off her thanks. "I thought I owed it to you to read her to sleep, seeing as how I'm the one who got her wired by bringing her to that restaurant."

Jolene waved away his notion. There was no need

to apologize for that. "Amanda was born wired. Well—" She looked toward the front door, her meaning clear.

Mac cleared his throat, then asked, "Would you mind if I asked you for a glass of water? My throat's a little dry."

Normally she'd hold the request suspect, but he had read to Amanda for over an hour, doing different voices. One of which had been particularly high and scratchy. She couldn't just send him off coughing. "Sure, come this way."

The kitchen, located at the back of the house, was no less cluttered than the living room had been. Maybe more so, given the boxes of appliances and pots and pans that still hadn't found a home.

Mac leaned against the sink as she ran the water. "How long have you been here?"

She knew he was referring to the clutter. Jolene handed him the glass.

"Six weeks." Her tone was a little defensive. It was hard being a nurse and a mother, much less an interior decorator. "I just haven't found the time to unpack."

That sounded reasonable. He took a long drink of water. "Need help?"

Oh, no, she wasn't going to have him volunteer to help her unpack her boxes. There was no way she was going to have him riffling through her things and she had no doubt that, with him, one thing would only lead to another.

"Need time," she corrected.

She was watching his every move as if she expected him to pounce on her. Mac set the empty glass down on the counter.

"All right, since my services are no longer needed, I guess I'd better be going."

He didn't have to say it twice. Jolene was already striding out into the living room. "Well, thanks for everything. Amanda had a great time."

He noticed that she said nothing about herself. Was that because she hadn't had a good time—or because she had and didn't want to admit it?

He stopped just short of the door. "Is this your version of the bum's rush?"

"No, I was just clearing a path to the door in case you forgot where it was." She pulled it open, waiting for him to go so she could finally let go of the breath she was holding. The one that was making her pulse race and her temples throb.

"I know where the door is, Nurse DeLuca."

Mac paused, looking at her. Wondering why, when she had done everything she could to block every one of his moves, he was still so damn attracted to her. It wasn't as if she was the only woman in the world, or that she'd even won his heart.

Just his determination.

He ran the back of his fingers along her cheek and watched in fascination as her pupils grew large. He leaned in just a little. Cutting off both their air supply.

"Aren't you the least bit curious, Nurse DeLuca?"

"No," she lied. Why wasn't she pulling back? Why wasn't she pushing him that last six inches over the threshold and slamming the door?

Why was she standing there like some pea-brained

possum, watching the headlights of the car coming right at her?

She hadn't a single plausible answer.

"Well, I am," he told her.

Tilting her head back ever so slightly, his eyes on hers, Mac touched his lips to hers.

And the earth was suddenly rocked with a second Big Bang phenomenon.

Chapter Nine

She'd meant to pull away, not be blown away.

Nothing seemed to matter but what was going on right here before her front door.

She was in complete and utter meltdown.

There was no other way to put it and there were a million things she could blame it on, not the very least of which was that she hadn't been with a man since her divorce.

Hell, she hadn't been with a man even *before* her divorce. Intimate relations had all but become non-existent between Matt and her since around the time she'd become pregnant with Amanda. That meant three years without being touched, without being made to feel special or feminine.

A woman had needs just like a man.

And MacKenzie was definitely stirring up her

needs, making them sit up and beg. Making her acutely aware of just how long it had been since she'd been made love to by a man.

How long it had been since she'd even been kissed by a man.

That was all that was responsible for her reaction, her logical brain insisted: needs, desires, random passions, nothing more. It had nothing to do with the man on the other end of her lips.

It had *everything* to do with the man on the other end of her lips.

Without realizing it, Jolene moaned, leaning her body in to his. Savoring the way it heated: instantly like a fire-eater's torch. Savoring the way MacKenzie pressed her to him, the hard contours of his body fitting against hers. Taking her a step higher.

Igniting the ashes that were left in the wake of the meltdown.

He'd known it. Known it the instant that he'd first seen her. The lady was definitely hot. Sex on toast once you got passed the waspish tongue and the attitude.

Mac felt a deep sensation of pleasure taking root and flowering within him as he slid his hands from her face and encircled her shoulders, bringing her closer to him.

The funny thing was, the closer he brought her, the more it wasn't close enough.

He wanted it all. He wanted to have her in her bed, nude and ready for him.

Hell, he would have wanted her right here, on the floor, if there hadn't been a little girl to consider. As much as the fire was beginning to rage within him,

Mac didn't want to take the chance of having Amanda wander down the stairs at an inopportune moment.

But there was the bedroom.

Still kissing her, his mouth slanting over and over against hers, he began to slowly guide her from the front door. His heart was pounding hard in anticipation, as hard as if he'd just spent a full hour working out in the gym with weights.

Except this workout promised to be a great deal more pleasurable.

Jolene felt desire scraping its nails across her, beckoning her onward. Urging her to draw this man back inside her house and take him upstairs...

Alarms suddenly went off in her brain, bringing her out of her revelry.

What in heaven's name was she doing? Running into the enemy camp, naked with a sign around her neck saying Take Me?

With the last ounce of willpower she could scrape together, Jolene pulled away. Her hands wedged against MacKenzie's chest, she pushed him back as if he'd been a volleyball just served over the net.

Her breath returned to her lungs in fits and starts. "Just what the hell are you doing?" she said accusingly.

For the first time in his life, he felt just the slightest bit shaky in his knees. The lady gave as good as she got. "It's called a kiss. If I have to explain it to you, it's been too long."

So what, this was now an act of charity on his part? He was the neighborhood Goodwill wagon, devoted to going around and lending out his lips and who knew what else to sex-starved women?

Not by a long shot, buddy.

Her eyes blazed. "It's called seduction and you don't have to explain a damn thing."

"Good." He reached for her. "I was never good with words."

She slapped away his hand. "Oh, don't act humble with me, MacKenzie. You are very good with words, and lips—and I'll bet everything else you came equipped with." He grinned at her and she could have scratched off his expression with her nails. Instead she took a step back from him. "But I am not in the market for a quick roll in the hay."

Very slowly, his eyes washed over her, taking long, languid measure. "I'm never quick."

More bragging. She didn't need to hear this. Didn't need the quick, heart-fluttering electrical impulse that was traveling through her at the very suggestion behind his smile.

"Save it, 'Harrison,' for one of your honeys."

For a second there, when he'd kissed her, he'd thought that perhaps she was ready to retire her dueling pistol. Apparently not. This obviously wasn't going to be the kind of night he'd envisioned just a few seconds earlier.

So be it. He could accept that, even though every fiber in his body cried out for satisfaction.

For her.

But he wanted her clear on something. He didn't like the image she'd just erected of him. It wasn't funny anymore. "I don't have 'honeys.'"

"Oh, please." Jolene rolled her eyes as she put as much distance as she could between them before she was tempted to fling herself back into his arms. She could feel her lips still throbbing. "Next you're probably going to tell me you have deep, meaningful relationships with every woman you sleep with."

He wasn't about to lie. Everyone knew commitment was not on his agenda. But neither was he after something tawdry just to satisfy an urge. To have her believe that would have been an insult to all the women who had been part of his life.

"The relationships are meaningful for as long as they last." He could see she was about to laugh in his face. "I don't do one-night stands, Nurse DeLuca, if that's what you're thinking."

She began moving around restlessly, angry at the way things had turned out. Angrier still at the way she'd caught herself wanting them to turn out.

"You don't want to know what I'm thinking." Jolene pivoted on her heel, suddenly facing him. "So what are they, then? Two-night stands? Maybe three? How many times do you generally sleep with a woman before you suddenly disappear?"

There was no rule of thumb, other than to call a halt to things when it looked as if they were getting too serious. He wasn't about to lead anyone on, no matter how enjoyable the sex.

"I enjoy women," he told her simply. "And they enjoy me." He had no idea why he felt he had to explain himself to her, or why he was bothering. But for some reason, it seemed important. "I've never forced myself on anyone, never taken anything that wasn't offered."

Was he telling her that she'd thrown herself at him? She fisted her hands at her hips. "Then what do you call what just happened here?"

For two cents, he'd shut her mouth the old-fashioned way...but then he'd be negating what he'd just said. So he kept his distance, wanting not to. ''Satisfying our mutual curiosity.''

She swallowed, suddenly feeling as if she was losing ground. ''I wasn't curious.''

If he didn't leave right now, he was going to break all his own rules and be the exact kind of man she was accusing him of being.

Mac opened the door, stepping over the threshold. ''All you had to say was no.''

Fuming, angrier with herself than with him, Jolene grabbed the door and slammed it in his face. ''No,'' she yelled at it.

She heard the sound of his shoes on the pavement as MacKenzie walked away, heard the car start. Turning from the door, she found she couldn't take a step farther.

Jolene leaned her back against the front door and slid down until she was sitting on the floor in a confused heap. So many conflicting emotions were running through her, firing shots aimlessly in the air.

She wrapped her arms around her knees, leaned her head against them and cried.

She felt like a woman on death row, waiting to walk the last mile, not knowing exactly when the door to her cell would even open. More succinctly put, she was waiting for her first hideously uncomfortable encounter with MacKenzie at the hospital after the fiasco of the previous evening.

With every hour that went by, though extremely busy, Jolene became more and more on edge. She hated the way she felt, hated MacKenzie for making her feel this way.

Damn it, why had she let him kiss her?

She'd gone over and over that in her mind during the wee hours of the morning, upbraiding herself, finding no answer that remotely satisfied her. Things were just not going to be the same at Blair, not while they were both working here. Not after that.

Stupid, stupid, she thought as she applied EKG tabs on an overweight man who had come in complaining of chest pains.

She credited MacKenzie for having enough sensitivity—or whatever he chose to call it—to realize that what he'd had before him last night was a woman who needed affection, who needed to feel desirable. He had all the training to carry that off with aplomb.

The rat had come at her like a homing pigeon at dinner time.

And if she let him make love to her, he'd undoubtedly do a fantastic job of it. And then go on to the next woman.

Attaching all the right wires to the right tabs, Jolene pressed a button on the machine and watched as a printout came oozing out of the portable EKG unit.

Remember what you learned from Matt.

The problem was, what she'd learned from Matt was to distrust every man with even an ounce of charm. And that wasn't the way she wanted to be, not deep down. She wanted to be able to trust people, both male and female, no matter what they looked like. She wanted to be normal, the way she had been when Matt had come into her life. She wanted to be full of hope and optimism and joy.

The way she'd felt for one thrilling moment when MacKenzie had kissed her.

"How bad is it?"

The patient's raspy voice quavered as he asked her, his small eyes watching the squiggles that were being printed.

She knew it wasn't up to her to give a prognosis, to say anything other than everything would be fine and leave it at that. But she hated seeing anyone in misery.

Jolene smiled at him. "Looks pretty good, Mr. Rand. The doctor'll be by in a few minutes to talk to you. You might just have a case of indigestion. That can get pretty nasty sometimes."

The man beamed at her, relief shining from every inch of him. "Really?"

"Really, but you might want to see a cardiologist just in case. Dr. Graywolf is on staff and he's excellent."

"Graywolf, huh?"

She nodded, taking the tabs off the corpulent man again and quickly returning them to their rightful place. "Lukas Graywolf."

"Thanks, I'll remember that," he called after her. Rand was still beaming.

"Oh, nurse, nurse, please, I can't get up and I need to go to the bathroom before I explode," the man in the next bed pleaded, trying to snare her attention.

Jolene turned. The patient, a man in his seventies, was hooked up to all manner of monitors. Getting up would require a huge effort and involve an incredible amount of untangling.

"Be right there," she promised. "Just let me put this away."

She pushed the EKG machine back to its place, then darted into the supply closet to get a urinal for the man in bed number seven.

There had to be a full moon out tonight, she thought. The E.R. was packed.

Walking out again, she saw MacKenzie walking in her direction. An urgent sense of self-preservation had her making a sharp U-turn and darting back into the closet.

This was ridiculous, she thought. She was a grown woman, why was she hiding in the closet?

Because she didn't want to talk to him, that was why. Not now at any rate. Maybe in a year or so.

And suddenly she didn't have a year. Or even a "so." The door was opening and she just knew MacKenzie was going to be standing on the other side of it.

She was right.

The serious expression on his face faded, replaced by the grin she had gotten accustomed to seeing on his lips as he looked down at what she was holding.

"Looking for donations, Molly Pitcher?"

Color flashed into her face. For a second, she'd forgotten all about the urinal and the man who needed it. She braced herself, sure that MacKenzie would try to detain her here until he had his say.

"Bed number seven is going to burst if I don't get to him."

To her surprise, MacKenzie stepped out of the way and let her pass. "Can't have that."

But then, to her dismay, he followed her out of the supply closet and back down the hall.

That's all she needed, to have him cause a scene. There was no avoiding it. She was going to have to have this out with him before they got back to the central floor.

Her heart pounding, she turned on him. "Look, about last night—"

Mac cut her off at the pass. "Yeah, I had a nice time. Your daughter's really a wonderful kid. She's a great credit to you. I'm assuming you raised her by yourself."

Again, he managed to floor her. Not expecting anything remotely close to what he'd just said, the compliment threw her completely off.

She wasn't even sure which statement she was answering. "Yes, I did. I am, but—"

"But?"

Jolene stopped, regrouping. Trying not to think about last night and the way he'd made her feel. Soft, pliant. Willing.

If this kept up, she had a feeling she was going to wind up her own worst enemy. "What are you trying to do to me, Harrison?"

Mac winced at the use of his given name. It had been his mother's maiden name. His family tree, if carefully traced, went back to both American presidents via a distant relative connection. That didn't make him dislike the name any less.

"Just trying to say thanks for last night, Nurse DeLuca." He paused, knowing that if he said "no," she would definitely say "yes." But he had to try. The woman had to have a kinder side to her somewhere. "Could you maybe find it in your heart not to call me Harrison?"

It really bothered him to have her use his first name. She had to admit she got a kick out of that.

"Maybe," Jolene answered loftily. "I'll think about it."

"Dr. Mac, could you come here a minute?" Mac turned toward the nurses' station and saw Wanda holding the telephone receiver over her head to get his attention. "There's someone on the phone asking for you."

"You'd better go answer that. It might be another eager date," she said sarcastically.

"Not on the hospital line." He made it a strict rule. That was what his cell phone was for. "Sure," he said to Wanda. And then he looked down at the item Jolene was still holding in her hand. "You said something about bed number seven exploding?"

Oh God, she'd forgotten all about the man.

Not saying a word, Jolene hurried away to bed number seven, hoping she wasn't too late.

She could have sworn she heard MacKenzie laughing behind her.

The first encounter had been less awkward than she'd imagined. The ones that followed that day were even less so. He was completely cordial, but no friendlier than he had been before they'd gone out. To her surprise and no small confusion, MacKenzie acted as if nothing had happened last night beyond the usual.

He acted as if there hadn't been all the ingredients for a spontaneous combustion.

Tired, she opened her locker and took out her purse. It was good to be going home.

Her thoughts shifted again.

Had it all been just her imagination, fueled by the fact that she had been almost devoid of all intimate contact for almost the last three years?

Or was he just being clever and laying a trap for her by playing with her mind? At a loss, she closed the door again and spun the combination around.

She had no way of knowing what was going on in his head. All she knew was that suddenly, a man she didn't want to even think about was on her mind a great deal of the time.

And she didn't like it.

Mac replaced the receiver in its cradle and leaned back in his chair, stealing a moment for himself. The chair, several generations old, squeaked in protest. He vaguely noticed.

It was all set.

The paperwork had all been approved, the hospital agreeable. He even had a pediatrician, Alix Ducane, standing by, just in case. Tommy's stepfather was bringing the boy in tomorrow to undergo the first of the surgeries.

Mac didn't think that more than three, possibly just two, would be required to fix the damage that had been done by the man's dog. A dog Allen claimed was now chained up in the backyard.

Mac made a mental note to drive by the house and check that out for himself if he could. He didn't particularly trust anything Paul Allen had to say. According to a friend he had on the Bedford police force, the man had been obedient when someone from animal services had gone out to check out the Doberman. He'd promised to keep the dog chained up outside and away from the boy.

Mac hoped that fear would work where logic and compassion hadn't.

Pushing himself away from his desk, he got up, wondering where the wisdom was in allowing children into the lives of people who didn't deserve them, or had no use for them. Sometimes he couldn't help wondering what God was thinking.

If it hadn't been for having two children, his parents wouldn't have remained together for more than a couple of years, if that long. Instead they'd stayed married until he turned eighteen, as if his age magically dissolved the sham that had been their marriage.

The more he looked around, the more he saw that marriage was just a shackle imposed by society in order to try to foster some kind of stability. Most of the time, all it did was foster discord before the marriage in question disintegrated.

Even Jolene was an example of that. She would have been a great deal happier if she'd never married her ex. Probably a lot less suspicious, as well, he was willing to bet.

Would he have been as attracted to her if she hadn't posed such a challenge?

He thought of the kiss the other night and had his answer. He definitely would have. There was no doubt in his mind that if she hadn't had her ex in her life, Jolene DeLuca still would have been one of the most attractive women he had ever seen.

And he was willing to bet that the way she kissed had nothing to do with her ex-husband.

Walking out of the small cubicle, he saw Jolene hurrying to one of the trauma rooms.

Speak of the devil.

Instinct had him picking up his pace and following her. Bursting through the swinging doors, he saw that there was a large man convulsing on the examining table. Activity hummed around the victim.

Standing at the head of the table, Lukas Graywolf was issuing orders.

Abruptly the man stopped convulsing. The monitor attached to him was flat-lining. Lukas called for paddles to be charged.

Mac raised his voice above the din. "Anything I can do?"

Paddles in hand, Lukas looked up and saw him standing just inside the doorway. "We've got it covered, Mac. But thanks."

Just before he walked out of the room, his eyes locked with Jolene's. He could have sworn he saw tears in them, but then she turned away.

Probably just a trick of the lighting, he decided.

He stood there a moment longer, watching her. There wasn't a moment's hesitation as she seemed to anticipate Graywolf's orders. "We've got a pulse," she declared with relief.

A strange feeling came over him as he watched her. If he hadn't known better, he would have said it was pride. But that was ridiculous. Pride was only there if strong feelings were present. There were no strong feelings here, other than attraction.

Mac walked out. He didn't have time to stand around and ponder things that made no sense. He had patients to see.

Chapter Ten

Mac stopped leaning against the wall and came to attention the moment Jolene walked out of the staff lounge.

He'd been waiting for her. The expression on her face earlier in Trauma Room Two had haunted him for the better part of his shift. She'd looked as if she needed a friend.

"Heading my way, Nurse DeLuca?"

Still preoccupied with what had happened earlier, and what had almost happened in the operating room less than half an hour ago, Jolene hadn't even seen him standing there.

Startled, she resumed her clip-walk down the corridor. It looked as if her streak of bad luck was continuing. She never slowed her pace. "I'm going to the parking structure."

He fell into place beside her, his long legs cutting the distance quickly. "Then you're heading my way."

Her mood was bad. She shot him an annoyed glance. Great, this was all she needed to top off a perfect day, to have him hit on her. "Don't you have anything better to do?"

His expression was guileless. "Not at the moment." Mac peered at her profile. He hadn't been mistaken earlier. Hers was clearly a troubled face. "Something wrong?"

She picked up her pace. "Yes, I'm being stalked by a doctor."

"Besides that." He followed her through the revolving door. "You look upset. More upset than I could make you," he added for good measure.

Guilt had all but eaten away at her ability to maintain her temper. "It's none of your business," she snapped.

If she was trying to push him away, she wasn't succeeding. Wounds of any sort spoke to him—on both a personal and professional level.

"Healing *is* my business." And then, less seriously, he added, "See, two ears, no waiting." The smile on his lips wasn't seductive or sensual, just coaxing. "You look like a woman who needs to talk."

The evening air was cool, bracing. She could smell more rain in the air. All she wanted to do right now was get away from him. "I don't want to talk—"

He let her get a step ahead of him, not wanting to crowd her. "I said needs to, not wants to."

She swung around to face him. It was on the tip of

her tongue to tell him that he could go, posthaste, to a southerly location, travel accommodations via a handbasket, but something stopped her.

Maybe it was the need he was talking about. Staring unseeing into the mouth of the parking structure, she took a deep breath. The guilt, the blame, just tumbled out.

"I almost killed him."

Mac took an educated guess. "The man in the emergency room?" He came up to her, resisting the temptation to put his arm around her in comfort. He knew she wouldn't take it that way, she'd take it as an advance. His hands remained at his sides. "What are you talking about? I saw you in there. You handled it like a pro."

She shook her head. "No, not today. The other day. He came in a few days ago complaining of chest pains. I did an EKG on him and told him he was fine."

Her admission caught him off guard. This was serious. "You diagnosed him?"

"No," she spat out, taking the question as blame. "I know my 'place,' Doctor. I just answered his question when he asked about the results."

Very carefully, Mac felt his way through the mine field. "It's not a matter of 'place,' but you should have left that for the doctor on duty."

Ready for a fight, welcoming it, Jolene fisted her hands on her hips. "I did. I told him the doctor would be by to talk to him. I even told him that he should see Dr. Graywolf, just to be sure." Damn it, she'd done everything right, why did it feel so wrong? "I didn't know he'd check himself out and just go home."

Only to be brought in by the paramedics his wife had called when she found him on the floor, gasping for air and clutching his chest.

The specter of what could have happened weighed heavily on her.

There was no point in lecturing her. She seemed to have taken care of that on her own. "What matters is that he's okay now."

Didn't he get it? Was he willing to whitewash everything just to get on her good side and crawl into bed with her? "But I could have killed him," she insisted heatedly.

A family, obviously visitors, made their way into the parking structure. Mac stepped aside to give them room, waiting until they passed to speak.

"No," he said patiently, "*he* could have killed him. You don't get a body like that overnight," he pointed out. The man was three hundred and fifty pounds if he was an ounce. "He'd slowly been killing himself for years and when he pressed you for answers, he just wanted to hear someone tell him that he wasn't."

It didn't make her feel any better about it. "And I came to his rescue."

"Yes, you did," Mac told her firmly. "You were part of the team that saved his life." He stopped, realizing he was taking something for granted. "You did save him, didn't you?"

She nodded. Otherwise, she didn't think she could have stood it. "He's in CCU."

The hell with playing it safe. Mac slipped his arm

around her in the most gentle way possible. One friend to another. "All right, then stop beating yourself up. You got a degree in nursing, not clairvoyance. Bad calls happen to all of us, even Super-nurses."

She drew in a long breath, then exhaled, trying to calm down, trying to gain perspective. She looked at him. This wasn't what she expected. "Why are you being so nice?"

A twinkle came into his eye. "I'm a nice guy, Nurse DeLuca. Haven't you heard?"

She tried to remember this was the man she'd been warned about. That this was the man who collected women's hearts the way others collected baseball cards. "I heard a lot of things."

His grin was quick, bright and went straight into her chest, unsettling her heart. Waking up butterflies sleeping peacefully in her stomach.

"Only the good parts are true." They'd reached her car. He paused, knowing she still needed to talk. And he still needed to help. "Feel like grabbing a cup of coffee somewhere? Or is your mother going out on another hot date?"

"Not tonight—"

His car was on the next level. He sank his hands into his pockets and took a step away from her. "All right."

She realized he thought she was turning him down. Something scrambled within her, telling her not to let him leave. "No, I meant she's not going out tonight."

"Oh?" He retraced his steps. "Then coffee would be all right?"

She couldn't seem to prevent the smile that came

to her lips. It was a continuation of the one she felt inside. "Coffee would be all right."

There was something slightly different about her now. More open. He decided to take a chance. "How about dinner?"

She opened her mouth to say no, to tell him not to push it. How the word yes came out she had no idea. But it did. Naked and vulnerable, but with its head held up high. And eager.

"Yes."

"Where would you like to go?" He thought of several places in the area she might like.

"Home first. I need a shower." She wanted to wash the last of her guilt away before going out with him.

My God, she was actually going out with him.

The thought struck her like a marble headpiece across her chest.

He could do with a change of clothing himself, he thought. "I'll pick you up in an hour? How's the Italian House sound?"

"Fine, but I'll meet you there."

She was still cautious, he saw. Well, Rome wasn't built in a day and neither was the road to Rome. Amusement teased his mouth.

"Separate cars, very independent and modern. Do we get to share the same table?"

"Yes." Funny, she didn't balk at his teasing the way she might have. Today had *really* shaken her up. "But all we do is talk."

He looked at her very solemnly. "I never make love in a restaurant. Doesn't go with the entrée."

Jolene heard herself laughing. It felt good.

* * *

Mac glanced at his watch. It was seven-thirty. He'd been sitting at the table, working his way through the bread sticks, for the last half hour.

Maybe she wasn't—

And then he saw her. Following in the wake of the hostess. Looking better in a simple light-blue dress than anyone had a right to. He half rose in his chair, feeling his knees lock into place.

The hostess left Jolene at the table with a menu and faded into the background.

Everyone did.

As far as he was concerned, Jolene was the only one there. "I was beginning to think that you'd changed your mind."

Jolene opened the menu, but although she skimmed it, she didn't see a word. She was suddenly acutely aware of the man sitting opposite her. Aware of how handsome he was in a light-gray suit, aware of the light scent of aftershave that seemed to burrow its way into her senses.

"Not about dinner, just about my clothes. I couldn't decide what to wear."

She could have come wearing aluminum foil and it wouldn't have mattered. He just wanted her there. "I'm flattered you went to all that trouble."

She didn't want him to think he had any more of an advantage than he already did.

"Don't be. I just couldn't remember where anything was packed." She took another look at the menu, trying to focus this time. "My clothes are still tucked away in three boxes."

"Only three?" he marveled. She really was unique.

"Most women I know would have had five or seven boxes—and that would be just for the weekend."

She looked at him pointedly. "Most women you know wind up naked."

He laughed, tickled, not taking offense even though he had a feeling she would have preferred to start something now. "I'll be sure to tell Wanda that next time I see her."

Jolene frowned. "You know what I mean."

"Yes, I do. And you're wrong." The woman was taking things way out of proportion. "If I had the kind of life you're crediting me with, I wouldn't have time to eat, much less operate."

She raised a brow in his direction. "I'm sure you operate just fine."

Out of the corner of her eye, she saw the food server approaching their table. Her stomach contracted at the same time, making her realize that she was starved, as well as nervous.

She welcomed the diversion.

She really hadn't expected MacKenzie to be as nice as he was.

All through dinner, she kept telling herself it was just part of his act, part of his plan to get her to lower her guard. But she'd driven her own car and was free to leave at any time, so maybe he really was as nice as he came across.

Or maybe he just wanted her to think this way.

By the end of the evening, her head was buzzing and it had nothing to do with the single glass of wine she'd had. She just wasn't sure about him or the way she felt, both earlier and now. She wasn't sure about anything except that she was still shaken up by the events of the afternoon and what she'd almost done.

To MacKenzie's credit, he'd done his best to talk her out of it, to patiently point out that, like it or not, she was like all the rest of them: human. Since the patient was still alive, it was pointless to dwell on what "might have been." The fact of the matter was, it hadn't "been." Graywolf had performed an emergency bypass and everything looked hopeful.

Mac signed the receipt the server had left at his plate and pocketed his credit card. "Would you like to come over to my place for a nightcap?"

She was hoping he wouldn't ask, because she *did* want to come over. That was the problem.

Discretion, she reminded herself, had always been the better part of valor. Since she was driving, she fell back on a standard excuse. "I'd better not. One drink is my limit."

He pulled out her chair for her. Old-fashioned manners. When was the last time that had happened? she wondered.

"I have ginger ale," he said.

He had his hand against the small of her back, guiding her through what had become a crowded room. Small, warm shivers were dancing in the wake of his fingers, bringing every part of her body to attention. And awareness. "You also have a very persuasive manner."

He smiled at her as he opened the door. "I'm counting on it."

Jolene bit her lip, debating. Knowing she shouldn't. She hadn't trusted MacKenzie before, what made her think she could trust him now?

"Just ginger ale, nothing else?"

"Unless you find something else you like—in my refrigerator," he qualified when she raised a brow.

There was a teasing note in his voice she deliberately overlooked. "Fair enough. You'll notice the operative word here is fair."

Taking her hand in his, he wove his way through the parking lot to where they had left their cars. "It always is."

Which was how Jolene came to find herself at his place.

MacKenzie's town house was located in a development that had only recently gone up, its proximity closer to the hospital than her own home. Commuting, for Mac, was something that took a matter of minutes.

Tall, stately, the three-story house was nestled in between two similar homes. The buildings gave the appearance of tall, thin soldiers standing shoulder to shoulder in formation at revelry.

Inside, unlike her house, there was a minimum of clutter. It was apparent that Mac didn't get involved with owning things. She wondered if the color scheme reflected his view of life. Everything was either black or white, including the walls, rug and furniture.

Keeping her purse close, contemplating escape even as she stood there, Jolene looked slowly around. "Don't you like color?"

He was already in the kitchen, opening the refrigerator. Because of the nature of the house, there were only two rooms per floor. The first had a living room and kitchen. The family room and formal dining area were upstairs. Mac maintained it allowed him to walk off his calories, going from one level to another.

"I found color was always difficult to match things to." He returned with a bottle of ginger ale and two glasses. Setting down the latter, he filled them. Ginger ale fizzed and sparkled like champagne as it made its descent into the glasses. "You can't go wrong with black and white."

She accepted the glass from him. "Very practical of you." Jolene studied him for a moment. "You don't strike me as the practical sort."

He laughed shortly, but there was humor in his eyes. "We already know what I strike you as—someone just above an amoeba in the evolutionary scale."

She almost choked on the sip she was taking, stifling a laugh. "No, higher than that."

"I've been redeemed?"

Feeling magnanimous, she gave him his due. "You're nice to children and nurses who mess up."

"I'm nice to everyone," he corrected and in general, he tried to be. Life was too short to bear grudges. He sat down on the sofa, urging her to join him by silent example. "Especially to nurses who mess up."

Very slowly, she sat down on the opposite end. Jolene cocked her head, wondering if she'd been all wrong about him. Or if the truth lay somewhere in the middle.

About the only thing she did know was that he had beautiful eyes. The kind of eyes that could look into a woman's soul.

Two seconds before they stole it.

"Because we're easy prey?"

He shook his head. Struggling with the urge to

touch her, he held the stem of his glass just a little tighter. "Now there you go again, making me sound like some kind of predator. I'm kind to nurses who mess up because I don't like seeing people down on themselves. Life's too short to dwell on what went wrong." His voice softened. "Learn from it and move on."

She looked up at him pointedly. "By those standards..."

He knew she was talking about her ex and that she was comparing the two of them. He wasn't quite sure why that rankled him, but it did.

Mac shook his head. "Not in the same league, not even remotely. I think cheating on your spouse is reprehensible. If you commit to someone, you stay committed. If you're going to give in to temptation, you don't get married in the first place. Which is why I think most people shouldn't."

He was so serious, it was hard not to believe him. Especially when he added the last sentiment. "Well, at least you're honest."

"Always." He prided himself on that. "No games—" his eyes held hers "—except interesting ones that involve bits of clothing removal at strategic times."

The laugh died in her throat as she looked at him. There was no denying it. She was irresistibly drawn to him and she could have sworn that somehow, the space between them on the sofa had shortened, even though she hadn't moved a muscle.

Suddenly aware of the very hum of the air between them, Jolene held her breath.

Mac took the glass out of her hand and placed it

on the coffee table beside his, his eyes never leaving hers. Her breath evaporated as he cupped her face in his hand. Tilting her head ever so slightly, he touched his lips to hers.

It was like falling headlong down a spiraling tube in slow motion.

The ache that rose up to seize her came a great deal faster.

The next thing she knew, there was no space between them and she was the one deepening the kiss. She was the one who slanted her mouth over his over and over again, burrowing straight into the heart of the kiss.

Her body felt as if it was on fire.

The same needs that had risen up before on her door step that night were back and they had brought friends. Scores and scores of friends.

Everything within her cried out for a union with this man.

Tawdry or not in the final analysis, she knew that while it was happening, it would be spectacular. A man who could kiss you as if the end of the world was imminent couldn't be a lousy lover. It just wasn't possible.

Mac hadn't intended for it to go this fast this quickly and that was just the trouble. He had a feeling that once this was over, Jolene would hate herself for allowing it to happen. And hate him for taking advantage.

He couldn't let that happen, even though wanting her had just jockeyed into all top five positions on his list of wants and desires. She was making his pulse race and the air in his lungs do strange things. It was like finding himself marvelously high without having a clue as to how or when the journey had even begun.

His body throbbed, pleading with that part of him that could still reason.

But he couldn't do this. Not to her, not to himself. Because if he took advantage of Jolene—and that was what he'd be doing—he wouldn't really like himself very much when it was over. He didn't believe in taking unfair advantage of anyone.

So with effort that bordered on the superhuman, he caught hold of Jolene's shoulders and, ever so slightly, pushed her back.

Dazed, disoriented, Jolene looked at him.

It surprised her that she still had her clothes on. She would have thought that they would have incinerated on contact.

Dragging air into her lungs, she waited so as not to sound like a simpering, breathless teenager. "What?"

"I don't think you want to do this." She would never know, he thought, how much it pained him to say this.

The last time she'd been this shocked, she'd found her husband with the receptionist "taking dictation" beneath him. "What?"

Mac got up from the sofa, because if he didn't, if he remained sitting where he was, he was going to forget all about the noble instincts he was striving to remember and go with the ones that were inbred.

Pacing, he ran an impatient hand along the back of his neck. "God only knows where this is coming from, but go home, Jolene."

He was calling her by her name. He'd never done that before. It made it personal.

Of course it was personal, she reviled herself. Her lips had all but had to be surgically removed from his.

Still something within her hoped that she misunderstood him. "What?"

The words burned in his throat as he pushed them out. "I said go home. Go home before I forget all about what I learned in the Boy Scouts."

Lots of words were flying around her head. She was only hearing one thing. "You don't want me?"

He laughed harshly. What was he doing, trying to be a Boy Scout at his age? "Not very intuitive, are you? Yes, I want you, want you more than I want to breathe right now, but I don't want this to happen for the wrong reasons."

She didn't know what to think. She only knew he was rejecting her after she was finally willing to give in. Needed to give in. "And those are?"

"Because you almost lost a patient today and you're feeling vulnerable. Because you want to get back at your ex. Because I'm pushing you."

But he wasn't, she thought. Not right now. Not if she was being honest. "I thought that was the whole idea, you pushing."

His eyes were serious as he looked at her. "I don't push. When it happens, it's mutual."

She squared her shoulders. "So you're sending me home."

There was something in her eyes that ripped open his heart. He'd hurt her. "For your own good."

She didn't need to hear excuses. "Okay. Okay,

fine.'' She grabbed her purse and strode to the door, wanting only to put this all behind her.

Then, surprising him and herself, she suddenly strode back into the room and kissed him. Kissed him harder than she'd ever kissed anyone before.

Stunned, Mac drew back his head to look at her in wonder.

''Maybe I don't want to be good.''

There was no maybe about it.

It was out of his hands, he thought. A man could only hold off so much.

Taking her purse from her, Mac let it drop to the floor.

Chapter Eleven

The words "stop" and "wait" echoed in the recesses of her brain, then faded away.

She didn't want warning cries, she wanted what Mac could do for her.

She wanted to feel again.

To feel that wild, exhilarating rush coursing through her veins, reminding her that she was alive.

Reminding her that she was a woman.

Not just a nurse, not just a mother, but a woman, a woman a man could desire.

Because Dr. Harrison MacKenzie wasn't just some loser sitting on a bar stool in the corner, praying that tonight he'd get lucky; he was a man who could easily have any woman he wanted. And he wanted her.

She'd been fending him off from almost the very first moment she'd met him, but she didn't want to fend him off any longer. At least, not tonight. Not now. Later would be time enough to go back to business as usual and to put this evening of passion and her misstep behind her.

Jolene wasn't doing this to be loved, or to lay foundations for "happily ever after." She knew there was no such thing as happily ever after. She was going into this fleeting liaison with her eyes wide-open, expecting nothing but a good time.

And more than anything, she knew that MacKenzie could show her a good time.

Now that she'd made her intentions clear to him, she half expected that he would have stripped her of her clothing faster than a top spinning around on its point. That had been Matt's way. With her experience limited to one man, Jolene assumed that every man followed more or less the same pattern, especially since MacKenzie had to know that foreplay was not of the essence. That she was a willing participant in this sensual dance they were engaged in.

But he surprised her again. This time by moving slowly. By lingering on her mouth as he caressed her, his fingers curving slowly along her body as if she was made of porcelain china.

Her head spun, her body heated not just to his touch but in *anticipation* of his touch. More surprises. *She* was the one who wanted to go faster, to scale summits quickly. Wanted to, but didn't. She was drugged by the power of his mouth, by the hypnotic sway of his body against hers as it molded itself to her.

An urgency for fulfillment fought with the desire to have this go on forever, building toward the final crescendo she suddenly craved with every fiber of her being.

Her fingers diving into his hair, she gave herself up to the delicious sensations battering her body and reveled in them as if this was the very first time for her.

Because, in a way, it was.

Mac had never kept count of the women in his life. Somehow that seemed tacky to him. But there'd been enough willing partners for him to know that this one was different, far more different than the others. Pacing himself took more effort than it ever had before because he wanted her with an urgency that beat hard and fast within him.

It had been a very long time since he'd felt like this, not since his teens.

Maybe not even then.

Creating a small pocket of space between them even as his mouth continued its assault on her senses, Mac began to undo the tiny buttons along the front of her dress, patiently separating each from its hole one at a time. His lips left hers and worked their way along her jawline and the hollow of her throat.

He could feel her quivering beneath his hand. Could hear her breathing increase, could hear his own become more audible as excitement began to roar through his veins.

An eternity later, he'd freed her of the material. A thrill swirled through him as he slid her dress from her shoulders, down her arms. It pooled around her feet.

She was wearing a teddy, something soft and sensual and sheer, with tiny blue flowers scattered wantonly against a black background.

He nearly swallowed his tongue just looking at her.

How could her husband have walked away from this? Even feeling the way he did about marriage, Mac couldn't understand someone willingly leaving a woman who looked like this.

It was as if somewhere, a gun had gone off, bringing her back to consciousness. Jolene realized that she was standing before him, almost nude, and he was still as formal as when he'd walked through the door.

Not for long, she promised herself. This wasn't going to be one-sided if she could help it.

Playing catch-up, Jolene had to concentrate to keep her hands from trembling as she pushed his jacket off his arms. She yanked it away, then tugged his shirt out of his pants.

Her fingers got in her way. Unbuttoning his shirt took a talent that she almost couldn't master.

She could feel him smiling against her lips. Rather than make her back away in flustered embarrassment, she pushed on with determination. ''I'm not used to undressing men.''

He drew his head back to look at her for a moment before forging on. She looked beautiful in this light, he thought. Like a proud goddess out to tame a beast.

And she was telling the truth. He could see that in her eyes.

''I'm glad.''

Mac had no idea where that had come from and he didn't want to think about the fact that he meant it. This wasn't the time to think, this was the time to steep himself in the sight, the feel, the smell of her. In all the sensations that this woman was causing to rise up within him like some kind of wanton tidal wave beating against the shore.

The clothes she ordinarily wore had only given the slightest hint of the body that existed beneath. She had a beautiful figure. Her waist was small, her hips firm and her belly taut and tempting.

He splayed his hand over it, his fingers brushing along her thighs. Her moan enflamed him.

They found themselves on the floor, a tangle of limbs and desires, explorers on the cusp of brand-new, undiscovered countries.

Anointing her skin with his lips and tongue, Mac began at her breasts and worked his way slowly, maddeningly down along her body.

The dips and hollows quivered as he took each part of her and made it his own.

Every fiber of her body felt as if it was screaming, urging him on, begging him not to reach journey's end too quickly. Jolene dug her fingers into the short pile of his white rug, twisting the strands just as her own body twisted in complete ecstasy.

She arched her back, all but levitating off the floor as Mac teased her into her first climax. The explosion she felt came suddenly, with bright lights shooting up and blotting out the darkness.

The sensation racked her body, stealing her breath and her mind away.

Before she could gather up her strength, he was doing it again, creating something out of nothing, bringing up a surge of energy within her when she could have sworn there was none.

This time the sensation almost undid her. She fell

back, barely able to drag air into her lungs, her thoughts obliterated.

And then she was suddenly looking up into his face. He was over her, his body sliding into place along hers provocatively.

The exhaustion she'd felt just a moment earlier was a thing of the past.

He smiled at her a moment before he brought his mouth down on hers. Smiled not seductively, but genuinely, as if everything was all right. As if she was safe from any and all harm forever.

She understood now why women gravitated to this man. Because more important than making them feel desirable, he made them feel good.

Mac framed her face in his hands and just looked at her for a moment. She was beautiful. So beautiful, it almost hurt.

He couldn't hold himself back any longer. Though the satisfaction he enjoyed in pleasuring her was immense, he needed to be one with her. Now, before he was completely torn apart by the needs that were all but consuming him whole.

Mac sealed his mouth to hers a moment before he entered her.

As his kiss deepened, so did the tempo of the rhythm he had initiated. The beat grew faster and faster until finally the uppermost point that they both sought was reached and conquered.

A euphoria of the magnitude he'd never encountered before enfolded him in its arms as he slowly felt his descent take hold.

All he could think about was holding Jolene to him in an effort to sustain this sensation, this feeling of incredible peace that had come from nowhere and overtaken him.

His heart still hammering hard, Mac rolled off her and gathered her to him, unwilling to break all connection just yet. Mac pressed a kiss into her hair as he waited for his heart to stop pounding like a drum and start beating normally again.

Well, she'd done it. She'd slept with the enemy and found him far from enemylike. What did she say at a time like this? Beyond "wow," of course.

She stared at the vaulted ceiling, her head resting against the downy hairs on his chest. The beat of his heart seemed oddly comforting although she hadn't a clue as to why.

"That was some nightcap," she finally said. She felt him laugh softly, the sound rumbling along his chest, teasing her cheek.

"At least you can't say I plied you with alcohol and got you drunk so I could have my way with you."

She raised her head slightly to look at him. "Did you? Have your way with me, I mean?"

He ran his fingers along her cheek, caressing the softness. "I'd like to think it was your way, too."

It was, she thought, and that was just the problem.

Time to get dressed and go, a small voice within her pleaded urgently.

She rose on her elbow, wishing there was something she could use to cover herself with beyond the growing pink flush of embarrassment.

She cleared her throat, looking away. "Well, I'll spare you any awkward moments."

She was going to bolt. Mac caught her wrist before

she had the chance to get up. He noticed how small and delicate it felt in his hand.

"Jolene, if I pushed you in any way—"

What kind of game was he playing? They both knew what had happened. "If I remember correctly, I was the one who grabbed you."

Yes, she was, he thought. She'd almost made it to the door, home free, and then she'd turned back. Luckily.

"Why?" Mac slowly traced the outline of her lips, watching her eyes as he waited for her to give him an answer.

She could feel her heart begin to step up its tempo again. This couldn't be good for her. *He* couldn't be good for her. He fell into the category of designer ice cream—and she was supposed to be on a diet.

At a loss for an answer, even to herself right now, she shrugged.

"It seemed like a good idea at the time." Damn it, he was making her skin dance beneath his touch, to say nothing of what was going on in her body further down. She tried to steal herself off and found she couldn't. "I wish you'd stop doing that."

This time, his smile was almost wicked as he looked into her eyes. "Why?"

"Now you sound like Amanda." Her daughter was always asking why until there were no answers left. This time, she felt as if she was starting off at that point. "Because you're making me..." Desire was causing her voice to fade away.

He leaned forward, touching his lips to her temple. "Making you what?"

"Want things again." The words were ushered out on a breathless sigh.

His lips teased hers, moving just along the perimeter. "Things?"

Damn him, he knew perfectly well what he was doing to her. He'd honed his act to perfection. "You, all right? Making me want you again," she answered tersely. "Does that satisfy your ego?"

"My ego—" he kissed her eyelids shut one at a time "—has nothing—" Mac proceeded to each cheek "—to do—" and then her chin "—with this." He claimed the hollow of her throat.

By the end of his sentence, he'd effectively disintegrated her thought process. What remained were the same smoldering desires that had already been uncovered once this evening.

It wasn't fair that he could do this to her and she was leaving him unaffected. "Then...what...does?" she managed to ask.

Mac stopped kissing her long enough to gather her to him again. His eyes held hers. "Guess."

Jolene could feel her heart fluttering in her chest. "I think I can get it on the first try."

"Be my guest."

Her smile worked its way up to her eyes as she laced her arms around his neck and brought his mouth down to hers.

Erika had dozed off reading one of the romance novels she so dearly loved. They'd been her diversion of choice ever since she'd snuck her first novel out of her sister's bookshelf at the age of twelve.

The sound of someone moving around downstairs woke her.

Her first thought was for Amanda's safety. She glanced at the telephone on the nightstand and thought of calling 911. But what if she was just imagining the noise? What if it was part of her dream? If the police showed up and there was no one, they'd think she was just a nervous old woman. She didn't much care for the old part of the label.

She was going to have to check this out before calling. Taking the baseball bat that had been her late husband's weapon of choice to use in case of a possible break-in, she cautiously made her way out of the room and to the top of the stairs.

Erika held her breath, then switched on the hall light. "I've already called 911, so you'd better get out of here before they arrive."

"Fine, but after I get Amanda."

Hand over her heart, Erika sank down on the top step, the bat beside her. "Jo, you scared me half to death."

Crossing to the foot of the stairs, Jolene looked up. "Didn't look that way to me from here." She eyed the baseball bat next to her mother. "Who were you expecting, Mark McGwire?"

Erika rose to her feet again, using the bat as leverage. She made her way down the stairs. "It's late, you never know."

"This is Bedford, Mother. Nothing dangerous every happens in Bedford." *Except for having Harrison MacKenzie making love to you,* Jolene added silently. "Sorry I'm so late."

That Jolene was here at all disappointed Erika. "I

didn't expect you at all," she told her daughter. She
attempted to read Jolene's expression, trying to dis-
cern how the date had gone without asking. "You
know, you could have stayed the night. All you had
to do was call."

Flustered, Jolene looked at her. She'd wanted nothing more than to stay the night with Mac, which was
exactly why she hadn't. "What are you talking
about?"

"I'm referring to that gorgeous man you were out
with tonight. I thought the two of you might—"

Because the two of them had, she didn't want to
hear her mother elaborate any further. "We went out
to dinner, Mother," she cut in quickly. "A person
can only eat for so long."

Jolene was being too evasive, too skittish. Erika
began to think that perhaps the date had gone well
after all. She smiled.

"You'd be surprised how long you can eat when
you've built up an appetite." The mother in her did
a quick evaluation. "You look tired."

The truth was, she was dead on her feet. The man
had amazing stamina. Her ex-husband's limit had
been once and then he usually dropped off to sleep.
She had a feeling if she hadn't had to go home,
MacKenzie could have kept going all night.

Relieved that she was in the clear, Jolene let her
guard down and sighed. "I am."

Erika's gaze swept over her daughter. Confirmation
came. She smiled broadly. About time. "Is he as good
as they say?"

Jolene's eyes flew open. "Mother!"

"What?" Of the two of them, it was obvious to

her that it was her daughter who was the prude. "I thought we could have one of those modern mother-daughter relationship where we could talk about these things like two adults. I do know where babies come from, you know. I was the one who told you."

Jolene pressed her lips together. All she had to do was hint at what had actually happened and she'd never hear the end of it. Her mother would be sending out wedding invitations by the end of the week.

"There were no unscheduled visits to cabbage patches, Mother."

"Too bad." Erika struggled to keep a straight face. "I think a trip to the cabbage patch would have done you a world of good."

Her mother never ceased to amaze her. When she'd been growing up, there'd never been a hint that this wild woman existed within her mother's skin.

"What are you saying? You *want* me to hop into bed with him?"

Erika touched her cheek lovingly. "I'm saying, dear daughter, that I want you to enjoy life." The soft smile became positively mischievous. "And he looked like a very enjoyable part of life."

She didn't need this. She was already feeling guilty over her lack of willpower. "Just worry about your own life, okay?"

Her green eyes grew very serious. "When are you going to learn, Jolene? You *are* my life. What hurts you, hurts me." She tried to shrug away the serious moment. "I think it has something to do with the umbilical cord, I'm not sure. But once you go through that process, nothing is ever the same. You're a mother, you should know that."

Her mother meant well, she knew that. It was her guilt at being untrue to her own principles that had her snapping like this. Jolene forced a smile. "Does that mean that you're experiencing everything by proxy?"

Erika considered. "In a manner of speaking." And then she couldn't resist. "So, did I have as much fun this evening as I think I did?"

Jolene merely shook her head. "Just get your granddaughter for me, okay?"

"Spoilsport," she murmured. "By the way." She indicated the front of Jolene's dress. "You missed a button.

Jolene flushed as she turned away and slid the button back into its hole. Exasperated with herself and the fact that her mind kept insisting on reliving the evening, Jolene dropped onto the sofa. Exhaustion caught up with her a second time. With a sigh, she laid her head against the pillow tucked into the corner. She'd just rest for a moment, just until her mother got Amanda ready.

She knew she should go up and help—and she would. In a second. As soon as she caught her breath.

Being with MacKenzie had completely drained her of all her energy. The man had made love with her three times before she finally summoned the strength to crawl back into her clothes. He had asked her to spend the night and for a second, she actually had considered it.

But she knew even as she was debating that she couldn't. Amanda was waiting for her. Motherhood wasn't a responsibility she could just put down and pick up at will. It was a 24/7 proposition and she had signed on for the duration.

Without thinking, Jolene closed her eyes, promising herself that she'd jump up in another moment and go help her mother get Amanda ready.

All she wanted was to close her eyes for just five minutes, close her eyes and not think of Harrison MacKenzie and the way he'd managed to set the whole world on fire without burning a single thing.

Except for her.

"Honey, I forgot to ask you if you wanted—" Returning into the room, Erika stopped by the sofa and smiled to herself. "He really did tucker you out, didn't he?" It was about time Jolene had a little fun and if she was any judge of character, that young man presented "fun" in capital letters.

Erika went to the hall closet and took out the afghan she'd made several years ago. It wasn't very good, but she'd kept it as a first effort. There'd never been a second one.

She spread the afghan over Jolene, careful not to wake her.

"I'll get up in a minute, Mom," Jolene murmured, her eyes still closed. She curled up under the cover. "Just five more minutes."

"Take all the time you want, honey," Erika told her softly. "I'm not going anywhere."

"Thanks, Mom." The words were all but sighed out as Jolene pulled the throw a little closer.

Smiling, Erika bent down and pressed a kiss to her daughter's cheek, then tiptoed away, feeling very optimistic about the future.

Chapter Twelve

"Looking for someone?" Reese Bendenetti finally asked after watching his friend's head bob up and down like one of those old-fashioned toy dogs. Mac had done it not once but several times in the space of the last few minutes.

The noise within the cafeteria was such that it took Mac a minute to realize that there was an unanswered question floating between them and that he was the one who was supposed to be doing the answering.

He looked back at one of Blair's top internal surgeons, a man recently engaged and destined to leave the ranks of the available within the next couple of months. Reese had even gone so far as to ask him to be part of his wedding party, something he was still contemplating, given his feelings about marriage.

Mac nudged the fare on his plate a little with next to no interest. "What makes you ask?"

"Well, for one thing, you're not paying any attention to your lunch. Not that, I grant you, the meat loaf merits much attention." Reese sighed. To him eating was one of life's pleasures. A pleasure that was currently being denied him. "I can't wait for Hannah to get back from her vacation." Hannah being Hannah Wong, the woman who did most of the cooking at the hospital's cafeteria. In the last five years, ever since she'd joined the kitchen ranks, she had almost single-handedly turned a standard joke into an appreciable dining experience for staff and patients alike.

"And for another," Reese continued, "you're not paying much attention to me, either."

There was no point in denying that he'd let his mind wander. He'd only heard about one half of what Reese had had to say since he'd picked up his tray at the entrance of the cafeteria and joined him.

"Sorry. And no—" he could be forgiven for indulging in a half truth, Mac thought "—to answer your question, I'm not looking for someone, I'm just thinking about this afternoon's surgery."

Which was what he should have been doing exclusively, Mac told himself, even though the procedure was a relatively short one on his side of the scalpel. On Tommy's side of the knife, of course, it was a huge deal. Any surgery at that age would be. Mac glanced up as someone walked into the cafeteria.

It wasn't her.

It made him a little edgy, knowing that he was looking around for her like this. It reminded him too much of a high school boy with his first major crush watching the doorway, waiting for the new girl to walk into his math class.

He was light years beyond that. So what was wrong with him now? How had she managed to crawl in under his skin this way when the thrill of the hunt was supposedly gone?

He purposely hadn't called her in order to make things appear light between them. They were supposed to be light—so why weren't they?

Mac looked down at his plate. He had no appetite. And even if he had, what he had before him wouldn't have satisfied him.

"You're right, this is pretty bad." He pushed his tray away. Then, for no reason at all, or maybe because Reese was one of his best friends, he reopened the topic. "You seen Jolene around? DeLuca," he added when Reese looked at him blankly.

The grin was instantaneous. Reese had had a feeling all along. "Oh, you mean the nurse from paradise. I think I saw her walking into the E.R. earlier." Two could play the vague game. "Why?"

"No reason." Rising to his feet, Mac picked up his tray. Deciding it was a good idea, Reese joined him. They walked to the conveyor belt that brought dirty plates and trays back into the kitchen together. "Well, I'd better see how Tommy's doing."

"Right. By the way, if I wasn't already spoken for, I'd be noticing her, too."

Mac thought it best not to comment on that. He wasn't even sure what had prompted him to ask Reese about Jolene, other than the fact that they were both on E.R. duty.

He was sounding more and more like that adolescent kid he'd never been, Mac thought, annoyed with himself as he parted company with Reese on the first floor.

Still, he looked down the hall before the elevator doors closed again.

It didn't surprise him that Tommy's stepfather wasn't with the boy in the pre-op area. The admitting nurse told him that Allen had brought the boy in, signed the necessary authorizations and then left, saying something about not being able to miss work.

What did surprise Mac was that the woman he'd been keeping an eye out for these last couple of days *was* in the room. When he dropped by to see how Tommy was doing, he found her standing over the little boy's bed, holding his hand and talking to him in a low, calm voice.

Just listening to her cadence did a great deal to calm *him.* As well as stir him, Mac mused, standing in the doorway and listening. A smile teased his mouth. She liked to come on tough as nails, but it seemed that the firebrand had a heart made out of pure marshmallow. It went a long way in her favor.

He caught Tommy's eye. Time to stop hiding in the shadows, he thought, walking in.

"Am I interrupting anything?" he asked the boy cheerfully.

Tommy kept his hand wrapped tightly around Jolene's hand. "Jo came by," he told Mac excitedly. "She's making me not scared."

"She's good like that."

"It was my break," she explained, banking down the sudden, flustered feeling. "I saw Tommy's name on the surgery chart." Why she felt compelled to explain her actions was beyond her.

Mac spared Jolene a smile before looking back at his patient. The scar on his cheek was no longer angry, but it was the first thing that drew attention.

Poor kid, he thought. There was no doubt in his mind that Tommy had endured a great deal of teasing these last few weeks.

Mac came around to the other side of the bed, purposely keeping a slight distance between himself and Jolene.

"You're not afraid, are you, Tommy? We talked about this. You're just going to take a short nap and when you wake up, your face is going to be a little numb and there'll be bandages on it, but we'll be that much closer to putting you back together again."

"With no scars?" Tommy asked hopefully, even though the ground had been covered before.

"With no scars," Mac assured him patiently.

Tommy licked his lips as he nodded, fear very much a part of the scenario. But if Dr. Mac said it was going to be okay, then it was. "And I'll look just like I did before?"

"Yes." He knew better than to make promises that wouldn't be kept immediately. "But not right away, remember?"

Tommy nodded solemnly. "I remember."

He couldn't resist ruffling the boy's hair. "Okay, then I'll see you in a little while in the operating room, okay?"

Tommy's eyes were as wide as saucers at the mention of his next destination. "Okay."

Jolene bent down and kissed the boy's cheek.

"Good luck, Tommy. I'll check on you after your surgery."

The nurse smelled good, just like his mother had, Tommy thought. And she wore a white uniform, too. It made his throat feel all scratchy and funny. He missed his mother a lot. Tommy looked at the man who was his friend. "Can Jo be there, too?"

She wasn't assigned to surgeries at Blair other than the emergency ones that took place on the floor of the E.R. "No, I—"

Having her there would probably go a long way in calming Tommy. Mac paused to consider. "Do you have operating room experience?"

She looked at him in surprise. "Yes, but—"

"Then you can be there if you'd like. I can arrange it." It wouldn't be that difficult, especially when all she would have to do was hold Tommy's hand and then not get in the way once he was put under.

She looked into Tommy's eyes. He squeezed her hand. "Please?"

Any hesitation she felt disappeared. "You clear it with Wanda, I'll be there."

"Consider it cleared."

The sound of guitars filled the operating suite, its tempo geared to keep the people within the room alert. It was how Mac wanted it, the way he conducted all his surgical procedures. To the sound of the Ventures wrapped in an endless summer.

Today the procedure was a relatively simple one, one of three that would eventually restore the boy's face to its original countenance. But Mac remained intently focused as he worked. He never took anything for granted in the operating room. To do so, to feel overly confident, even with the simplest of procedures, would have been an invitation to a mishap, a mistake waiting to happen.

The entire surgery took forty-five minutes from start to finish. Done, Mac left the brightly lit operating salon and stripped his gloves off. The mask followed. Glancing toward the swinging doors that led to the hospital corridor, he saw that Jolene was already out and on her way back to the E.R.

He pushed the door open and hurried after her.

She was immediately aware of him. "I didn't think you chased after anyone."

"I do if they bolt."

"I wasn't bolting," she corrected. "I was returning. To the E.R. I work there, remember?"

She paused, knowing she was becoming testy again. But that was because she couldn't stop thinking about him and she didn't want that happening, didn't want to find herself in the same position she had once been in.

Won't happen, she promised herself.

But somehow, the silent words seemed to carry less weight than they had the last time she'd vowed them.

"That was nice of you to arrange for me to be in there with him," she forced herself to say. And it was true. He kept doing nice things like that. It made it difficult to mentally keep sticking warning labels on him when he behaved this way.

"I try to make my patients happy whenever possible," Mac told her simply. "You made him feel calmer. He likes you." They were right outside the

E.R. doors. Mac stopped walking. "He's not the only one."

"You needn't practice your charm on me, Doctor." Jolene looked around to make sure no one was listening before she added, "We already know you can slide into home base."

"Maybe—" his smile was teasing, making her warm "—but it's just the beginning of the season."

She wasn't sure just what he meant by that. But before she could ask, she saw Mac looking down the hall and shaking his head. He blew out a breath, disgusted. "You'd think the guy would be out here after the operation."

She knew he meant Tommy's stepfather. It bothered her, too, but she'd come to be realistic about the roles some men played in their children's lives. Or didn't play. "Not everyone's a good parent."

"No, I guess not," he agreed. He would have liked nothing better than to shake some sense into the man's empty head. "Well, I'd better use my 'considerable charm' and see if I can get Administration to agree to allow Tommy to remain here at least overnight."

Normally cases such as the boy's were discharged within a number of hours, the patient sent home with a list of dos and don'ts to follow. There wasn't much chance of their being followed, he guessed. Allen had already proven he didn't care about the boy's well-being if it interfered with his own life.

"It goes without saying that bastard isn't going to be changing Tommy's bandages for him." Mac knew his limits. The hospital wouldn't spring for two nights. Not unless he hid the boy in the supply closet.

"Although I'm not sure what one night's going to do. That's going to take a week of care—"

She was already ahead of him. "I could stop by Tommy's house after hours. You know, like the Visiting Nurses."

He was aware of the group, nurses who were sent to render minor services to shut-ins. In this case, there would be no way to justify writing a prescription to cover the paperwork end of it, especially since there was no insurance involved. "It'd have to be on your own time."

She looked at him pointedly. "Didn't ask for compensation, did I?"

"No, you didn't." His mouth curved. There was something exceptionally tempting about her right now. "I could pay you in trade."

She'd had no intentions of there being a repeat of their date. Was almost adamant about it when she'd gone over it in her mind—time and again, just to make sure there would be no slipups.

Yet she heard herself asking, "Just what did you have in mind?"

Whenever a procedure went correctly, there was always this accompanying burst of energy with it that flowered all through him, giving him a sense of happiness, peace and purpose. It was overshadowed by what he was feeling now and he couldn't even begin to explain why since work had always been paramount in his life.

"Why don't I stop over at your place around seven tonight and I can show you?"

Not a good idea.

The words telegraphed themselves through her

mind with the urgency of a sinking ship sending out an S.O.S. She knew she should listen to it.

Jolene gave it a halfhearted try. "I've still got unpacking to do."

He wasn't about to accept any excuses. "Then you can use an extra pair of hands."

She couldn't help looking at them and remembering the other night. The way his hands had felt along her body. Touching her. Possessing her. "Depends on what those hands are doing."

The grin was unabashed. "Absolutely anything you want them to."

She flushed, turning on her heel. "I've got to get back to E.R." Jolene pushed open the door, then stopped and looked over her shoulder. "Seven-thirty."

That's all he wanted to hear. "With bells on."

"Wear more than that," she advised. "My neighbors talk."

The sound of his laughter followed her into the E.R. It warmed her for a considerable amount of time.

Her initial plan was to put Amanda to bed before MacKenzie got there. But that entailed something just this side of major warfare and Jolene was running short on energy. Besides, perhaps having the little girl around might be the better way to go. There was safety in numbers. Even short ones.

Though she tried to tell herself she was imagining it, there were definitely nerves jumping around all through her. They'd taken up residence in her stomach and were making friends with the butterflies that already lived there.

She needed, Jolene decided, to keep busy. Very busy. So busy that she wouldn't think about the fact that she was actually walking back into the lion's den and doing it willingly.

As long as she remembered that it was a lion in that den and not a pussycat, Jolene told herself firmly, she was going to be all right. This was a fling, nothing more.

She had to keep that uppermost in her mind. Otherwise, she was toast.

"Book, Mama, Silly book."

Amanda was standing before her, her tiny hands fisted on her waist, looking like a pint-size miniature of herself, Jolene thought. It was hard not to laugh, but she managed. Amanda had been following her all around the house ever since they'd come home, begging her to find one of her favorite books.

Always at the worst time, Jolene couldn't help thinking. She'd already checked every place she could think of where the book might be hiding. She'd unpacked it when they'd first arrived and placed it God-only-knew-where.

She tried to appeal to the little girl's sense of fair play, knowing she was hitting her head against the wall.

"I'll find it later, honey. I don't know where it is now." She knew why Amanda was being so insistent. It was the latest Silly Sandy adventure and ever since she'd told her that Mac was coming over tonight, the little girl had begun pleading for her to find the book. She wanted Mac to read it to her at "be'time."

So far, the search had been fruitless. She'd unpacked so many things in the last few days, working whenever she had a free moment, that she couldn't remember where she'd put the book.

"Now," Amanda pleaded. "P'ease?"

The only thing to do was to begin at the beginning and look for it again. Jolene found the thought daunting. But it was even more daunting listening to Amanda plead in three different octaves of whine.

She ran her hand along her neck, glancing up toward the bookcase.

And then she saw it.

The thin, light blue covered book was on the top shelf of the bookcase, tucked into a corner.

Whatever had possessed her to put it there? She didn't have a clue.

It didn't matter. What mattered was that she'd found it.

"Missed it completely," she muttered under her breath. She looked around for the ladder she'd used when she'd dusted the shelves and then put the books away.

The ladder wasn't in the garage where she could have sworn she left it.

Amanda haunted her tracks like a mischievous, dancing shadow. "Find it?"

"The book, yes, the ladder, no. Now that's missing." Jolene sighed as she walked back into the living room. "You know, Amanda, the next thing's that's going to go missing is my mind."

With another sigh, she improvised and grabbed a chair. It wasn't tall enough for her to be able to reach the top shelf, but if she placed the telephone books that had arrived on her doorstep last week on the seat and stood on her tiptoes, she could just about make it.

Why would she have put the book that high up? Jolene wondered again, positioning the chair before the bookcase. Obviously she hadn't been thinking.

She was doing a lot of that these days, she thought. There was no other explanation for allowing Mac back into her life. She didn't need sex that badly.

Oh, yes, you do, a little voice whispered.

Feeling color creep into her face, Jolene shut the annoying little voice out. "Once more into the fray," she muttered under her breath.

Amanda stood beside the chair, her arms raised. "Gimme."

Jolene glanced down reprovingly. "That's 'thank you,' not 'gimme,'" she corrected.

Bracing herself against the shelf, she stood up on her tiptoes, her fingers just brushing against the bottom of the book. Maybe she needed an extra phone book, she thought.

And then she heard Amanda declare, "Kitty!" like a battle cry. She looked down and saw the stray kitten they had adopted two days ago when it had shown up on their doorstep. It darted under the chair. Amanda was trying to grab its tail to pull it back.

Either the cat or Amanda hit the chair, jarring it. Jolene found herself airborne.

The last thing she remembered was hitting her head on the base of the fireplace.

Mac pressed the doorbell again. He'd already rung twice and was beginning to get a little concerned. The lights were on inside the house, but no one was answering the door.

Had she changed her mind?

But she wouldn't just leave him standing here. She wasn't like that. Besides, there was no reason for her to do an about-face.

Maybe she was experiencing the same quakes of uncertainty that he was, he thought. The ones that almost had him picking up the phone and calling her to cancel at the last minute. Cancel because he wanted to come here too much. But that was irrational and he liked to think of himself as a rational man.

Mac knocked this time, hard. Jolene's car was in the driveway, so she hadn't left, unless someone had picked her up.

No, she would have called, he insisted. Unless something had happened to Amanda—

He stopped himself before he could get carried away. Deciding on trying another approach, he took out his cell phone and called her number. The phone inside the house began ringing. No one was picking it up.

He was going to get the answering machine, Mac thought.

And then he heard a childish voice on the other end of the line.

"'lo?"

"Amanda?" He peered into the window, trying to look inside. But he couldn't see her from his vantage point. "This is Dr. Mac, is your Mommy around?"

"Mommy sweeping."

"Sweeping?" Why would she be cleaning? And then he remembered the little girl had a lisp. "Oh, you mean sleeping.'' That made no sense, either. Why would Jolene be sleeping if she was expecting him?

"Uh-huh. Sweeping. On da floor."

Maybe Amanda did mean sweeping—unless—

He had a bad feeling about this. "Amanda, can you open the front door? I'm right on the other side. Just turn the latch—'' She probably didn't know what that meant. Mac tried again. "The round thing above the doorknob—'' Did she even know what a doorknob was?

Frustrated, he knew that none of the words he'd used probably made any sense to the little girl. How did he describe what he wanted her to do so that she could understand?

Mac regarded the door before him. It was solid and there was no way he was going to break it down in the fine old Western tradition of John Wayne. The only thing he'd break doing that would be his shoulder.

The window, he thought suddenly. He could break the window and get in that way. It would probably frighten Amanda, but right now, that was beside the point. He had this uneasy feeling that time was of the essence.

Hurriedly taking off his jacket, Mac wrapped it around his hand. He was just about to swing it through the side window when the front door opened.

Amanda stood there, her hand resting on the latch, looking very proud of herself. "I watch Mama," she told him.

He grabbed her and kissed her quickly on the forehead. "Don't ever do that for anyone else," he instructed, hurrying into the room.

He didn't have to ask where "Mommy" was. Jolene was lying on the floor in the living room, face down and unconscious.

A panic swept over him. "Oh God," he groaned, rushing to her.

"See," Amanda said importantly, "Mama sweeping."

"Yes, Mama sleeping, honey," he said softly. He knew it was important not to scare her. Mac quickly felt for Jolene's pulse. It was strong. Good. Very slowly, he rolled her over onto her back. There was blood matting her bangs.

Jolene moaned.

There was a terrible throbbing weight pressing down on her head and her eyes felt as if they were sealed shut. Jolene struggled to rise above it, to open her eyes. Her baby was alone.

She had to get to Amanda.

With superhuman effort, Jolene forced her eyes opened, feeling like she was physically pushing up her lids. And they weighed a ton.

She fought against the urge to sink back into oblivion and let the darkness cover her.

Someone was touching her.

She could feel hands moving gently, competently all over her, her arms, her legs, her neck. What was happening? Where was she?

It hurt her head to breathe.

With effort, she drew air in just as the hands moved

along her rib cage, first one side, then the other. Pressing, testing. They hurt.

She realized that despite her best intentions, she still hadn't managed to open her eyes. She tried again. This time, she succeeded.

MacKenzie.

"Might have known," she mumbled, weakly trying to push his hand away. "Don't waste any time, do you?" Each word took effort to expel. Each word banged around in her head like so much noise in an echo chamber.

He assessed the wound on her head. It was a gash, but it didn't look serious. Wounds around the face tended to bleed a lot. "What happened?"

Jolene felt foolish. She wasn't supposed to do dumb things like this. "I took an unexpected flying lesson. I flunked. I'm all right, don't fuss," she mumbled.

Pushing his hands away, she drew her elbows in to her sides and tried to sit up.

And fainted again.

Chapter Thirteen

When she opened her eyes again, she was no longer on the floor. Instead she was on the sofa. MacKenzie was sitting on the edge of the coffee table, looking very concerned as he regarded her.

"I didn't think you were the type to faint at my feet."

"I'm not," she said weakly. She tried to sit up, but this time, Mac restrained her. Hands on her shoulders, he pressed her back down gently but firmly. Her spirit was willing, but right now, her flesh wasn't, so she didn't put up much of a fight.

There was something on her forehead. Gingerly she tried to examine it, only to have Mac deliberately take her hand away.

"Don't touch that. As a matter of fact, don't move until I tell you."

She wanted to ask him who he thought he was, but the words wouldn't form. Her head was throbbing too hard.

To her surprise, her exuberant daughter approached her with caution, looking more subdued than she'd seen her in a long while. Amanda turned her big green eyes up at Mac. "Mama aw right?"

Mac swept his hand over the little girl's head. Just seeing the unconscious display of affection brought an ache to the pit of Jolene's stomach.

"Yes, sweetheart," Mac told Amanda, "Mama's all right." He looked at Jolene sternly. He'd righted the chair and pieced together the story when Amanda had shown him her new kitten. You'd think that a woman with a degree in nursing would know enough not to try to stand on a shaky pyramid of phone books. "At least she will be once I get her to the hospital."

Jolene was immediately alert. "Hospital?"

He nodded. This was standard procedure. Why did she look so surprised? "I want you to get a Head CT, make sure everything's all right."

She wasn't about to go anywhere. "Everything is all right, I don't have to go to the hospital."

His expression was reproving. "Practicing medicine again without a license, Doctor?"

Jolene didn't take the reference to her recent error in the E.R. with grace. Her temper flared. "I know my own body."

He knew that tone. Unless he was willing to carry her out, kicking and screaming, she wasn't about to listen to him.

"Well, I'm just getting to know it and I want to

be sure it's not damaged.'' He fanned out his fingers before her eyes. "How many fingers am I holding up?''

''Your whole paw.'' Jolene swatted his hand away. "I'm fine," she insisted. "I just did a half-gainer off the chair, I didn't plummet off a bridge into the Pacific Ocean.''

Mac scrutinized her carefully again. Her pupils looked to be normal, so for now, he decided to opt for peace and leave the subject alone. But he intended to keep an eye on her, just in case.

''Well, the good news is that it doesn't look as if you'll be needing any stitches, so my surgical expertise won't be needed.'' After he'd cleaned it, he'd used a butterfly bandage he'd found in the medicine cabinet on the wound. Mac pretended to regard her face for a moment. "I could, of course, give you a new nose.''

She tried to focus on the appendage under discussion and immediately regretted it. Her headache kicked up a notch. "What's wrong with my nose?''

''Nothing.'' As far as noses went, it was rather well shaped and appealing—just like the rest of her. "But people are always thinking they need a different nose, or a better chin, or higher cheekbones, or any one of a number of other so-called improvements.''

''I don't want any improvements,'' she informed him. "I'm happy with my body just the way it is.''

Because she was hovering around, Mac scooped up Amanda and placed her on his lap so that she could face her mother and not be a moving target. "Good, so am I.''

There was no way she was up to cooking, and going out wasn't something she felt up to at the moment. So much for their date.

"I guess you'll be leaving now." Jolene flushed. She hadn't meant to sigh, but it had just come out, accompanying her words.

"I guess I'll be staying now," he contradicted. "I've a patient to watch and from the looks of it—" he lightly bounced Amanda on his knee; the little girl giggled "—a little girl to take care of." He set Amanda back on the floor and rose. "Have you eaten?" he asked Jolene.

She'd skipped lunch to visit Tommy and had eaten an apple while trying to get ready at home. "I was just about to throw something together."

Spoken like a modern woman, he thought with a smile. None of the women he knew, with the exception of Dr. Alix Ducane, could cook worth a damn. He looked toward the kitchen. "Why don't I take care of that?"

He was an endless source of surprise to her. When she'd talked about him, Rebecca had never mentioned that he knew his way around a kitchen, only a bedroom. "You cook?"

He winked at her just before he went into the kitchen. "I can throw something together with the best of them."

They had eggs Benedict and Mac insisted on cleaning up. All she had to do, he told her, was eat.

"You'll get no argument from me," she told him. "I know a good deal when I see one."

The glance he gave her sent ripples through her abdomen. "So do I."

Finished, he wiped his hands on the kitchen towel

and then took Amanda's small one in his. It was close to nine o'clock.

"I think maybe it's time I read that book of yours, what do you think?" A vigorous bobbing of her head met his question. "Funny thing about that book. I heard the story is better if anyone under three feet is wearing pajamas when they hear it. Want to give that theory a try?" He knew that Amanda couldn't have understood half the words he used. It warmed his heart that she agreed so readily.

Picking up the book that had started it all, he glanced back at Jolene. "I'll be back in a little while. In the meantime, don't fall asleep. That's an order."

Jolene sat down on the sofa, using the remote to turn on the TV. "I know all about head wounds, Doctor."

He noticed that this time her voice had a smile in it instead of offense. Mac figured he had to be making progress. The thought brought an unconscious smile to his lips.

It never ceased to amaze him how much comfort children derived from repetition. For him, everything always had to be new, fresh. Amanda had been thrilled to hear every word of the story spoken endlessly over and over again. It had taken almost an hour to read her to sleep. He'd almost succumbed himself.

Returning to the living room, Mac sank down on the sofa beside Jolene. He had a glass of water in his hand.

She'd been debating going upstairs to investigate,

wondering if he'd been the one to fall asleep instead of Amanda. Seeing the glass of water, she smiled.

"Thirsty?"

He raised the glass slightly. "I was going to toss it at you if you were asleep. But since you're not, I think I'll make use of it myself." He consumed nearly half the contents in one long gulp. His throat was completely parched. Setting the glass down on the coffee table, he looked at her. "How many times do you generally read *Silly Sandy Meets Mighty Mandy* to her?"

His having endured multiple readings bonded them more than working at Blair did. She laughed, picturing him being held captive by Amanda's plaintive "p'eases."

"More times than I'd like. In her defense, she hasn't heard it for a while." She looked at him, trying to gauge his limit. "How many times did you read it?"

"Five before she finally dropped off." He'd begun to think he was doomed for all eternity, stuck in a time warp reading the same sentences over and over. "I think I can recite the damn book by heart." To prove it, he leaned back, closed his eyes and began, "It was a big, beautiful October day—"

"No, stop, please." Laughing, she tugged on his shirt to get him to open his eyes and shut his mouth. "That's torture above and beyond the call of duty—"

Sitting up, he threaded his arms around her. The color had returned to her cheeks. He guessed he was just overreacting earlier. Other than the bandage over her eye, there was no indication of the fall she'd taken. She looked fine.

And he wanted her.

"You want torture, lady?" Mac gathered her to him, nuzzling her neck. "I can show you new meaning to the term sweet agony."

She could feel the pinpricks beginning all over her body. Her eyes held his. "I bet you can."

The doctor in him was afraid that he was allowing his needs to get in the way of his professional judgment. He looked at her closely.

"Are you sure you don't want to go to the hospital, Jolene? We can have your mother come over to watch Amanda—"

She rolled her eyes. "That's all my mother needs to hear, that I fell off a chair. She'll be here in a flash, lining the floors with foam rubber in case I ever trip or fall again."

It would have been nice to have parents who worried about you instead of spending their time, sniping at each other. Jolene didn't know how good she had it. "Maybe she just wants to make sure you're safe." He pressed a kiss to her hair. "Like I do."

Didn't he have any idea what he did to her? "Don't do that."

He wasn't following her. "Do what?"

"Be nice." She could handle the situation when he was being flippant, or sexy. But when he was being nice, the way he had been with Amanda earlier, she could feel herself being reduced to the consistency of ice cream melting in the sun.

"Sorry, occupational habit," he apologized with a definite lack of contrition. "I could beat you if you'd like."

She pretended to fend him off, her hands before

her. "No, thanks, I've seen you with a punching bag."

"That's right, I forgot." Ever so slowly, he began to stroke her side as he spoke. "I'm a lot better with a real live person."

She could feel her breath beginning to back up in her lungs. Just like last time.

"Yes," she said hardly above a whisper, "I know that, too."

Maybe he was taking unfair advantage, he cautioned himself. He gave her every chance to back away. "Do you want me to go?"

It would have been wise to say yes. She had the perfect excuse, that she was tired and sore and needed her rest. But she didn't feel very wise tonight. She felt a whole different range of things she didn't want to put into words, didn't want to examine.

And so, her answer was, "No."

He kissed her very, very gently, softly as if her lips were made of flower petals that would be crushed at the slightest pressure.

The longing that filled her was almost unbearably sweet.

She could hardly hear her own voice above the pounding in her ears. "I won't break, Mac."

"Just making sure."

And then he gathered her into his arms and rose from the sofa.

She looked at him in wonder, thrilling to the feel of being in his arms like this. She felt weightless. "Now what?"

"Now I'm taking you to your room." He turned

toward the stairs. "I feel the need for a more thorough examination coming on."

She laced her arms around his neck, feeling giddy and more light-headed than her fall would have made her. Her eyes danced as she asked, "How thorough?"

He kissed her before answering, his lips brushing quickly, urgently against hers. "Not an inch of you is going to be left untouched."

"Sounds promising."

He grinned, feeling the excitement beginning to mount. "And I always keep my promises."

He pushed open the door to her bedroom with his shoulder, walking in. Laying her gently on the bed, he was surprised when she grabbed his shirt front and pulled him to her. She raised her head and sealed her mouth to his.

If he meant to proceed gently with his lovemaking, his plans were doomed to go awry as she yanked them out of his hands and effectively burned them using just the heat of her mouth.

He had no reason when it came to her. It was like his mind was an empty echo chamber, with only her name resonating in it. Had he been able to think clearly just then, the fact that she could do this to him, to reduce him to this state, would have worried him. Always before, the second time with a woman, though pleasurable, was never as exciting as the first. It was a matter of record, a given.

Except for now.

Now there was even more excitement, more anticipation than there had been the first time, because now he knew what to expect and in knowing, wanted more. Wanted to steep himself in the tastes, the feel, the very scent of her.

But even as all these desires warred within him and this new terrain was uncovered, the doctor in him struggled to rise up one last time.

"You're sure you feel up to this?" He searched her face for an answer she might not want to admit to. "I don't want to hurt you."

I won't let you, she promised him silently, but even so, she had a feeling that it was already too late for the promise to be completely true.

Her mouth teased his as she kissed first one corner, then another. He made her feel well. The headache she'd had just minutes earlier had faded like a bad dream. "You're the one who's going to be hurt if you stop now."

She'd convinced him and Mac laughed at the threat. "Ah, a tough woman. Want to see how I handle a tough woman?"

Jolene arched her body against his, creating delicious waves of anticipation through it. "I'm counting on it. And by the way, actions speak louder than words."

He stripped his shirt off and began to undress her. "Your wish is my command."

If only, she thought.

If only.

But now wasn't the time to have regrets, to let herself think of what wasn't and what wouldn't be. Now was only the time to think of what was and to enjoy it to the utmost before it was gone.

The instant they were both freed of their clothing, she seized his mouth, determined this time to leave a burning impression on him that would last for the rest of his life.

The way he had already done with her.

Because in that one night of lovemaking she'd had with him, he had completely erased the nine years she'd spent with Matt, making them not only history, but a pile of smoldering ashes.

As her body heated, an urgency strumming her loins, she pushed him back against the bed and straddled his hips. Jolene could feel his desire growing against her. It gave her a sense of power and yet at the same time, filled her with a sweetness, a generosity of spirit that took her breath away.

She'd never felt this way before, never wanted to give of herself for the pure pleasure it created within someone else.

Everything Rebecca had told her about MacKenzie was true. And more.

More. She wanted more. She wanted forever.

The thought frightened her more than she could hope to put into words. She knew she couldn't have what she wanted—couldn't have him. She could only hope to have the moment.

She made the most of it.

Slowly Jolene lowered her body to his, purposely brushing against it ever so slightly and tantalizing him with each movement. She reveled in the look in his eyes, in the feel of his hands as they slid up along her ribs and over her breasts.

And then she carefully moved over him, taking him into her. She began to sway, first slowly, then with more and more urgency.

Her fingers dug into his shoulders. The rhythm of

lovemaking increased until it swept them both over the edge.

She moaned, savoring the explosion, savoring the feel of him. And then, very slowly, she sank against Mac's chest, her hair pooling along his torso, her body all but liquid.

And then, when she could, she raised her head and looked at him. Mischief outlined her lips. "See? I'm fine."

Mac tangled his fingers in her silky hair, cupping the back of her head. Holding her in place.

"Oh lady, you're so much more than fine."

Still joined in the most basic of ways, he surprised her by reversing their positions. She was flat on her back in less than a heartbeat. He drew back, creating just the smallest pocket of space between them.

Without a word, he began to take the inventory he'd promised, using his lips rather than his hands to examine every part of her.

She twisted and turned beneath his hot lips, absorbing every sensation that racked her body, craving more. Afraid that more would drive her over the edge again. She climaxed so quickly, she hardly knew what was happening before she was in the midst of its grip.

Shuddering, she had to bite her lip to keep from crying out.

Pleasuring his partner had always heightened lovemaking for him, but he had never felt it to this extent before. Never felt the level of satisfaction as he did from bringing her to this special place where only the two of them resided.

Hearing her moan his name as she twisted and

turned beneath him filled him with awe. With an over-whelming sense of happiness.

Scary stuff, a small voice echoed somewhere in the far recesses of his mind.

He shut it out by sealing his mouth to hers and letting the passion overtake him.

And when he had taken her a third time in as many hours, Mac hadn't the strength to draw himself away from her body.

Not the strength, nor the desire. He liked the feel of her heart hammering against his. Of remaining within her, two bodies joined in a warm feeling.

This is how it's supposed to be.

He had no idea where the thought came from and was too tired to chase it down. To chase it away.

With a sigh, he rolled off her, then gathered her to him.

Don't get too complacent, too comfortable, Jolene warned herself, trying to steel off the sensation per-meating through her.

She sighed softly, her breath moving the hairs on his chest. "So this is what you call a thorough ex-amination."

She could feel his grin. "Yup."

Slowly she stroked his chest, loving the feel of it. "You do this for all your patients?"

Mac raised his head to look at her, wondering if she was just teasing, or asking him something. And if she was, did he want to answer? He settled on the camouflage of banter.

"Just the special ones."

"I see. And what do you bill this under?"

She felt the laugh rumble through his chest, beneath her cheek. "Miscellaneous."

She sighed, contentment sweeping her into its arms, just as Mac had done a moment earlier. "Great word, miscellaneous."

It was the last thing she said before she drifted off to sleep.

The headache woke her, an annoyingly disconcerting sensation that buzzed around on the perimeter of her head, moving here, stomping there, marking its territory with a heavy foot.

She rose, picking up her robe from the floor where it had fallen last night. She was truly surprised that the whole bed hadn't collapsed. They had gone at it pretty vigorously.

The memory made her smile and nearly cut through the headache.

Nearly.

Entering the bathroom, she eased the door closed behind her before opening the medicine cabinet. The bottle of aspirin was on the bottom shelf. Putting a tablet in her mouth, she cupped her hand and caught enough water to help slide down the pill. She closed her eyes and hoped it would do the trick.

Glancing at the mirror, she shook her head. She looked like death. The least she could do was brush her hair. Grabbing a hairbrush, she pulled it through her hair, then frowned. Hopeless.

When she emerged out of the bathroom, Mac was on his side, his head propped on his hand. He was watching her.

"Everything okay?"

No, everything wasn't okay. But she wasn't about to share that. It was just a headache and it would go away. She didn't want him making a big deal of it. There were other ways she wanted him to play doctor.

"Can't a woman go to the bathroom without being questioned?" she replied flippantly.

He watched her approach, the folds of her silk robe rubbing along her body. "Got another question for you."

She stopped beside the bed and looked down at him. "And that is?"

He raised his eyes to her face. "What are you wearing under that robe?"

"Why don't you take it off and see?"

He was already reaching for the sash. "Is that a challenge?"

She felt him tugging at the sash. "Is that what you like, challenges?"

"I've been known to take up a few in my time." He yanked the sash away. Her robe fell open, framing her nude body.

She liked the way desire flared in his eyes. "And is that what I was, a challenge?"

Rising in bed, naked as the moment he came into the world, Mac pushed the robe from her shoulders. "In the beginning."

Her body sizzled from just the merest touch of his lips against her skin. "And now?"

He couldn't tell her just how much he felt. That would bind him to her. He kept it light. "Now you are the woman who lights my fire."

"Big talk," she scoffed, letting herself be drawn into the bed.

He grinned. "Bigger action."

She felt herself melting, but tried to hold back a second longer. "Show me."

Mac pulled her into bed and onto her back. "Thought you'd never ask."

His body covered hers.

Chapter Fourteen

Rebecca Wynters had been friends with Jolene ever since they'd been in the same math class together in their freshman year at Bedford High. Older by almost six months, Rebecca had always felt protective of the more diminutive woman. So when it began to look as if Jolene was seeing the legendary Dr. Mac outside of the hospital halls, she took it upon herself to go right to the source and state her mind.

She found Mac coming out of the E.R., about to go on a well deserved and extremely abbreviated break.

Accustomed to having women barrel down on him, Mac smiled a greeting as Rebecca followed him to the stairwell for the one short flight down to the cafeteria and a mug of life-affirming coffee.

"Hi, Becky, how's it going?"

She waited until the fire door had sealed itself shut behind them before saying anything. "You know, of course, that if you hurt her, I'm going to have to come after you and cut your heart out."

Mac stopped in the middle of the stairwell to look at the woman. The warning was given only half in jest. He didn't have to ask who she was talking about. Jolene had been on his mind almost continuously, a fact that did not cease to amaze him each time he became aware of it. It had never been his style to dwell on a woman.

Apparently styles changed.

Rebecca looked at him, her smile fading, her expression turning serious. "She's not like the rest of us, Mac. She's fragile."

He thought of how hard it had been to get past Jolene's guard. "Right—for a gunnery sergeant," he quipped.

Rebecca knew Mac better than most of the women he'd been with. Knew the kind of man he really was beneath the good looks and charm. Incredibly decent. After they'd gone their separate ways, her mother died and she fell into a depression. It was Mac who'd been there for her, Mac who had seen to it that she got help and rejoined the living. And Mac who had told her at the end to just keep everything between the two of them. He'd said if word got around, it would blow his reputation.

"You know what I mean." They began walking down the stairs again. "That's just Jolene's facade. She got a raw deal with that guy she married. Matt Jeffrey never met a woman he didn't want. She was so in love with him, she never saw it coming. Makes a girl think twice before handing out her heart again.''

Reaching the basement, Mac pulled open the door for Rebecca, his interest suddenly piqued. ''What makes you think Jolene's handed out her heart?''

Normally, just considering the possibility that a woman was becoming serious would have been a signal for him to pack up his tent and make an exit.

But the need to flee just didn't seem to be there. What was there, instead, was something akin to permeating sunshine, its rays reaching out in all directions. What was going on with him?

He looked at Rebecca, curious. ''Has she said anything to you?''

The corridor leading to the cafeteria was empty this time of day. Their voices echoed.

''It's what she hasn't said that gives her away.'' Rebecca paused at the entrance. She was still on duty and needed to get back upstairs. ''Be good to her, Mac. She's one of a kind.''

Rebecca would get no argument from him on that score. ''I already know that.''

She began to leave, then stopped and turned around again. ''Oh, and more thing. We never had this conversation.''

He looked at her innocently. ''What conversation?''

Rebecca laughed and quickly brushed her lips against his cheek. ''That's what I always liked about you, Mac. You always played by the rules.''

The only problem was, Mac thought as he walked

into the cafeteria, he no longer knew just what the rules were. Someone had changed them on him when he wasn't looking.

Pulling into the driveway, Mac yanked up the emergency hand brake as he turned off the motor. He was struggling to keep his temper in check. It wasn't easy. He shouldn't have to be doing this.

Allen hadn't brought Tommy into the hospital today as promised. They'd had a twelve-thirty appointment to discuss the boy's next surgery. Mac had purposely arranged for the appointment during the man's lunch hour so that Allen wouldn't shrug it off, saying that he couldn't take any time off.

Fat lot of good that had done. He'd waited until one. Allen had never showed.

The boy was getting more attention from strangers than from his own stepfather. Immediately after Tommy's last surgery, Jolene had been as good as her word and stopped by every day after she got off duty to check on the boy's progress. The surgery had healed nicely. And now it was time for the second procedure.

Except, Mac thought, frustrated, he couldn't put things in motion if there were no papers signed, no date set for surgery.

Too bad they didn't believe in public floggings anymore. Allen would certainly be his candidate for a horse whipping.

Mac got out of his sports car, slamming the door. So much for trying to calm down. Maybe he should have brought Jolene with him to keep him in check.

Even at a time like this, the thought of her made him smile.

Taking a deep breath, he composed himself and rang the bell. A dog in the backyard began to bark loudly. At least he was still keeping the animal away from Tommy, Mac thought. Maybe it just took time.

And then again, maybe not.

"You again." Allen regarded him malevolently. Dressed in a faded T-shirt with a tear on one shoulder, and a shapeless pair of dirty chinos, the man stood blocking the doorway. "What do you want?" he demanded curtly.

To hit you over the head with an unabridged copy of an etiquette book for starters.

"You missed your appointment," Mac said evenly.

Allen gave no indication of moving out of the way. "Yeah, well, I was busy."

Mac returned the other man's glare. "It was your lunch hour."

Allen shrugged, glancing over his shoulder at the television set blaring in the background. "Man's gotta eat."

He wasn't here to argue about the past. He was interested in the present. "I'd like to see him." It wasn't really a request, but more of a thinly veiled command.

Allen planted his legs squarely before the doorway, his arms crossed before his sizable chest. Everything about his stance made Mac think of a schoolyard bully who had never grown up.

"Look, am I gonna have half the damn hospital trooping through here? Your nurse's already made a pest of herself, coming by every night for more than a week. Don't you people ever back off?"

Mac felt the hairs on the back of his neck rising in response to the offhanded remark about Jolene.

"She believes in going the extra mile." Mac's eyes grew to small slits. "You might stand to learn something from her."

Allen smirked as he regarded him. "I bet she taught you plenty."

Mac could feel his fingers curling into a fist. The urge to sink it into Allen's face was almost overwhelming. But he wasn't here to defend Jolene's honor, he was here to try to mend a small boy's self-esteem.

He looked over Allen's shoulder into the room. "Where is he?"

"How should I know?" Allen snapped, tired of being put on the spot. "Around. I'm not his nursemaid." He went to close the door again, but Mac stopped him. Allen glared. "Look, that nurse said he was doing okay the last time she was here—"

He had explained all this to him when Allen first came to the hospital to sign the papers. Was the man being deliberately obtuse? Or just a pain in the butt?

Mac decided it was the latter. "He needs a second operation."

Allen was tired of hearing about it. The boy had been nothing but trouble from the first. "Well, I need a lot of things I'm not getting, either. It's a tough life." Again, he tried to close the door.

Mac stopped him, gripping his wrist tightly, his eyes full of loathing as he looked at the other man. "I can have you up on charges of negligence so fast your head'll spin."

"Negligence?" Allen spat. He gave up all pretense.

"Yeah, I neglect him. I don't *want* him. His mother died on me. I don't have time to waste raising him. You're so worried about the kid, you take him. I never adopted him, so he's not legally mine. You want him?" Allen jeered. "I'll make you a present of him. He's yours."

Mac saw a movement out of the corner of his eye. When he looked, he saw Tommy pulling back out of view behind the entrance to the living room.

The boy had heard everything.

Mac squelched an almost overpowering urge to pummel Allen to the ground. His heart spoke before his mind had a chance. "Yes, I want him."

For a split second, Allen looked speechless. And then he laughed. It was a harsh sound. "Then take him. Take him and get the hell out of here." He turned and yelled into the room. "Hey kid, get out here! You've got yourself a new old man." When Tommy failed to appear, Allen raised his voice. "I said get out here!"

Tommy came out hesitantly, his eyes wide, his gait halting as he looked from one man to the other. Fear was stamped across his small face.

There was no doubt in Mac's mind that if he left the boy here now, Allen would take out his foul mood on him, doing even more damage to Tommy's soul than to his small body. Mac couldn't leave him.

That he wasn't prepared to take on the responsibility of a child never entered into his decision. He simply reacted to what he saw, what he felt. Tommy needed someone and Mac wanted to be that someone for him. He'd grown to care a great deal for the boy in a very short time.

Planting the flat of his hand against the other man's chest, Mac pushed his way into the house. "Get your things, Tommy, you're coming with me."

The little boy sitting in the passenger seat beside him had been very still, very quiet the entire way. It was as if Tommy understood that once again in his all too young life, he was going through a life-altering change.

Mac had tried to draw him out, asking Tommy questions, but all he got in response was either a nod or a shake of the head.

He looked afraid, Mac thought. No child should be afraid.

It wasn't a long trip.

Pulling up in the driveway, Mac quickly got out and rounded the hood, then opened the door for Tommy. Taking his hand as the boy got out of the vehicle, Mac brought him to the front door of the Tudor-styled house.

He had nowhere else to turn to for help.

The headaches were coming more and more frequently. Haunting her until she fell asleep, springing out at her first thing in the morning, before her eyes were even opened. Plaguing her all through the day. There seemed to be little or no respite from the pain.

She bought herself a little respite each time she popped aspirins, but she found she had to up the dosage and the strength.

It couldn't go on like this, she thought, taking an almost empty economy-size bottle of extra-strength aspirins out of the downstairs medicine cabinet. She'd bought the bottle less than a week ago, she thought.

The doorbell rang. Now what?

Jolene tossed three tablets into her mouth and washed them down quickly. One of the tablets felt as if it had gotten caught in her throat on the way down.

Terrific.

Muttering under her breath, she hurried to the front door.

She wasn't expecting MacKenzie tonight. Hoping, maybe, because he'd taken to coming over unannounced, bringing excitement with him like Christmas in July. But even as she hoped, she told herself she was playing a dangerous game. A game that she would only lose if she expected to win.

Peering through the peephole, her heart did a little leap as she saw Mac.

Not a good sign, she thought, if her heart could still leap at the sight of a man she'd been sleeping with. This was casual, just casual.

Opening the door, her smile turned to a look of surprise.

"Hi, I wasn't expecting you tonight." Her eyes swept over Tommy who looked up at her shyly. "Either of you. This is new," she murmured to Mac, nodding at the little boy attached to him.

For possibly the first time in his life, words eluded Mac. "There's been a new development."

"I see." She extended her hand to the little boy. "Would you like to come inside?" She could hear Amanda coming down the stairs. Or rather hopping down them. Jolene glanced to make sure the little girl was holding onto the banister the way she'd been instructed. She was. "I've got some hot chocolate and a bouncy playmate you might like."

"So what's going on?" Jolene asked Mac once she'd situated Tommy, with his mug of hot chocolate, in her family room and introduced him to her daughter. The two hit it off instantly, with Amanda taking charge.

Amanda, Jolene firmly believed, was a born dictator looking for her own country to boss around.

Standing off to the side, watching her daughter slowly drawing Tommy out, Jolene turned toward Mac, waiting for an answer.

"I'm not sure." Looking back, it was all almost a blur to him. Mac shrugged. "Tommy's stepfather just gave him to me."

"*Gave* him to you? What do you mean, like a gift?" Although, from what she'd seen of Allen, she wouldn't have put something like that past the man. She'd never seen anyone so devoid of any feelings for the child he'd been entrusted with.

Mac blew out a breath and nodded. "Something like that." He knew he should begin at the beginning so she could make some sense of this. God knows he couldn't. "I went over there because Allen missed the appointment I'd set up to discuss Tommy's second reconstructive surgery. When I got to his house, Allen told me he had no time for that, that the boy wasn't really his responsibility and that if I cared so much, I could have him." Just repeating the scenario rankled Mac all over again.

Jolene laid a gentling hand on his arm. She could read the anger in his eyes. "So what are you planning to do?"

He dragged his hand through his hair. He wasn't prepared to be a father, had never even remotely thought about having children, but what choice did he have? Tommy was alone. Sometimes things just arranged themselves. Tommy was alone and he didn't want him to be. He wanted to be part of Tommy's life. Forever.

"I don't know. I asked Wanda about Tommy, she knew his mother best. She said that the woman told her she had no family, that was why she stayed with Allen even after he became abusive. If he washes his hands of Tommy, then Tommy goes into the system."

They both knew what that meant. Being passed from foster home to foster home until he was eighteen. "Unless someone adopts him."

"Unless someone adopts him," Mac echoed. He looked into the room again, watching the boy. Tommy looked so small, so defenseless. "I guess that someone would be me."

Jolene studied his face in silent. "You're really serious?"

"I said it. I guess I must be." Tommy laughed, drawing his attention. It was the first time he'd ever heard the boy do that. It was a nice sound. "I can't stand seeing a kid in pain."

Raising up on her toes, she kissed his cheek. He looked at her, surprised. "You know, you really never cease to amaze me."

Mac grinned at her cockily. "You mean outside the bedroom?"

She shook her head. He wasn't fooling her. There was a good man beneath that facade, even if he didn't want to broadcast it.

"That didn't amaze me. I expected that. Your legend preceded you." She looked at Tommy again. This was such a huge undertaking. "But taking in a child…"

He read between the lines, knowing what his own parents would have said about the situation had either of them still been alive. "I must be crazy, right?"

"No, you must be very, very nice." Taking his face between her hands, she kissed him softly.

A sweetness filled him. Mac rested his hands on her waist, drawing her to him. But now was neither the time nor the place to give in to the attraction he instantly felt each time their bodies were close.

Instead he held her to him, absorbing her warmth, telling himself he was doing the right thing. "Jolene, I hate to ask, but—"

She looked up at him, finishing his sentence for him. "Could he stay here tonight?"

Mac looked at her, clearly stunned. "How could you know I was going to ask you that?"

She laughed. "Clairvoyance comes nine months after the gestation period. Take a look, it's in the motherhood bylaws."

She was being incredibly understanding. He felt a little guilty, imposing on her this way. After all, this was his problem, not hers.

The fact that he was sharing it with her, or even considered sharing it with her, was not lost on him. "You don't mind? I need to get a few things, get a room ready for him, a bed—"

He didn't get it, did he? In a way, that made him almost modest. "He adores you. He'd sleep on floor at the foot of your bed like a puppy if you let him, but no, I don't mind," she added in case Mac thought she was changing her mind. "Amanda and Tommy probably won't sleep a wink until dawn, but that's okay. And tomorrow, I'll have my mother come over here to watch them."

He'd forgotten about that. He was going to need a baby-sitter, or a good day-care center until Tommy started school. "She won't feel put-upon, watching two?"

"My mother loves kids, the more the better." Jolene caught her lower lip between her teeth and worked it for a moment, thinking. "You realize this is a very serious step you're talking about taking and that there's going to be a great deal of red tape to wade through." She had no personal dealings with social services, but knew that the path was littered with overworked, underpaid people and paperwork.

"Probably less red tape than we think." He knew any action he took would be unopposed. He lowered his voice, not wanting Tommy to overhear. "Allen can't wait to be free of him."

She wasn't thinking about Allen being a problem, but there were other factors to deal with. "They're still going to have to check you out."

One of the doctors he knew had a cousin who worked for social services. The man owed him a favor. "I can pull a few strings."

She laughed, shaking her head. It was going to take more than that, but if anyone could do it, Mac could. "From where I stand, you're going to have to be a fully accomplished puppeteer, but somehow, I think you can pull it off."

For a moment, everything else took a back seat to

the woman beside him. Mac pulled her into his arms, thinking how right she felt there.

When had all this happened?

He obviously hadn't been paying enough attention. "Now I know why I came here."

She cocked her head, a smile playing along her lips as she looked at him. He almost made her forget the headache that was threatening to return, full force. "To be flattered?"

"No, just to be near you." God, but he wanted to make love with her tonight. "You make me feel good, Jolene."

The admission surprised her, but she warned herself not to make too much of it. He was just talking, nothing more. And maybe he was being grateful for her help. "So now I'm your drug of choice?"

There was something in her tone that told him not to let everything out, not to share with her these feelings that were milling about, holding a meeting within him. Entirely new feelings that were somehow involved in this whole new set of circumstances he found himself in.

So he said evasively, "Something like that."

And how soon before he tired of his drug of choice and went to sample another? Distance, she schooled herself. Distance was the key. As long as she remembered that he was at heart a man who couldn't commit, couldn't settle down, she'd survive.

But if he couldn't commit, what was he doing with Tommy?

Apples and oranges, Jo. Tommy is a good deed,

Tommy doesn't cut into his ability to move from woman to woman. It had nothing to do with her.

Her head began to hurt again.

Jolene hadn't realized what a terribly claustrophobic experience having an MRI could be.

It had taken her a week to work up the courage to finally go see the chief neurosurgeon on staff at Blair. She knew the man by sight and by reputation, but hadn't had any dealings with him before this.

Howard Monroe had surprised her by being warm and kind, reminding her a little of her grandfather who had passed away when she was nine.

Right now, though, the expression on his face didn't inspire optimism.

Clad in a hospital gown that made her feel incredibly vulnerable, Jolene sat on the edge of the table, trying to brace herself. "I'm not used to being on this side of the examining table."

His smile was kind when he looked at her. Was that pity? "They say doctors and nurses make the worst patients."

She bit her lip, nodding at the X-ray sheet he held. It was comprised of multiple views of her brain. "It's not just my imagination, is it?"

He put the large sheet on the rack and flipped on the illuminating light beneath it. "No, it's not. You have an aneurysm." He pointed out the area on several views. It looked no more than a pinprick. "Whether it was brought on by the fall, or the fall just activated it, I'm not sure, but it most definitely is what's causing your headaches." He switched off the light and placed the sheet on the desk. "You were right to come in when you did."

Jolene folded her hands before her. "I came in because I was hoping you'd tell me it was all in my head—so to speak."

He wished he could give her a clean bill of health, but they both knew better. "I'm not going to sugarcoat this, Jolene."

She raised her chin. "I don't want you to."

"You could continue for a long time like this, or it could get worse." He looked at her, seeing denial in her eyes. A common recourse, but she had too much going for her to take that route. "Want my advice?"

"That's why I'm here." She did her best to sound cheerful.

"Have the operation. The sooner you have that pressure relieved, the better."

That wasn't what she wanted to hear. She wanted him to assure her that if she did nothing, that would be all right. That somehow, the aneurysm would disappear on its own as mysteriously as it had come. "But I could go on like this, right?"

"Right." But it was a path best not followed. He'd taken the time to acquaint himself with her background before he'd come out to speak to her. "You're a single mother, correct?"

Her throat suddenly felt dry. "Yes."

"Your daughter's how old?" He knew the answer, but he wanted to have her hear herself say it.

"Two."

"Want to see her graduate elementary school?"

She blew out a shaky breath. She didn't want to deal with this, didn't want to have to face it. She was twenty-eight. That was too young to face her own mortality. "Now you're scaring me."

"Good, then I've done my job." He placed his hand over hers. "If you were my daughter or wife, I'd force you to do it."

She didn't want to go under the knife. What if she didn't wake up? What would Amanda and her mother do then? "But there's a downside."

He would have been lying if he said there wasn't. Every surgery came with risks. "There's always a possible downside. But chances are you'll come through it with flying colors. And not having surgery guarantees you a downside."

She felt tears clawing their way up her throat. "I don't have time for this."

The irony of her words coaxed a sad smile from him. "No one has time for an aneurysm, Jolene. They just happen. But if you want more time in your life—" She knew what he was going to say. Afraid she was going to break down in front of him, she looked away. "All right, I'll think about it."

He nodded. That was all he could ask. "Anyone you want me to speak to?"

"No." She shook her head adamantly. She would be the one to tell her mother. Eventually. "Absolutely not. This is just between you and me."

"Not even Mac—?" He paid attention to hospital gossip with half an ear whenever he needed amusement. He'd heard her name coupled with the plastic surgeon's more than once recently. He had a deep respect for the young man and his work ethic.

Jolene looked up at him sharply. "Especially not Mac. We're just friends, anyway."

He looked at her for a long moment. "Whatever

you want. But this isn't the kind of thing that you should deal with alone.''

She forced a smile to her lips. ''I'm not alone.'' Jolene blinked back the tears that were threatening to emerge. ''I have you.''

''Jolene—''

''I've done a great many things alone in the last few years, Doctor. I'm tougher than I look. And if I need to fall back on someone, I've got a great mother—who is absolutely going to freak out when she hears this, so I think I'll just keep this under wraps for a while if you don't mind.''

He had another appointment to get to. He began to leave the room. ''Just as long as you don't leave it that way for too long.''

Too long. That had such a finite, terminal sound to it. ''I understand.''

He looked at her pointedly. ''I hope you do. I'll have Rita schedule an appointment for you—'' he began briskly.

She didn't want to deal with that just yet. With appointments and the surgery that loomed at the end. Or the possible consequences that might arise. She needed time to absorb what he'd just told her. ''I'll get back to you on that if you don't mind.''

She was frightened. He didn't blame her. He knew every tactic taken by a frightened patient. ''Don't call us, we'll call you?''

''No, no, I'll call,'' she said slowly. ''I just need some time, that's all.''

He nodded. ''Understood. Just don't make it too long,'' he cautioned again, closing the door behind him.

She waited until she was sure he wasn't returning and then let the tears come.

Jolene gave herself exactly five minutes to cry and feel sorry for herself, then she squared her shoulders and got dressed. Lunchtime was almost over and she had to get back to the E.R.

Chapter Fifteen

Finding people to cover for him, Mac took the next few days off in order to make arrangements for the entirely unexpected turn his life had taken.

He'd gone to his sister for advice about a permanent sitter to watch Tommy during the hours when he worked. Jake Madison's cousin still worked in social services and he'd gotten the man's help in order to begin filing all the necessary paperwork that would eventually assure him of the boy's guardianship.

The process, though streamlined, still turned out to be a lot harder than Mac had anticipated.

But taking the boy into his heart had been easier than he'd ever have thought possible.

Mac had never entertained the idea of fatherhood before, not even fleetingly. Kids were part of marriage and the latter was never going to be part of his life, so there was no chance of the former. But when fatherhood suddenly appeared without warning on his doorstep, he found himself slipping into the role effortlessly. And with pleasure.

Just like he'd slipped into this relationship he had with Jolene, he realized.

He'd become accustomed to having her within his day, within his mind. Whenever odd little things cropped up in the course of his day, he'd find himself wondering how Jolene would react.

Or he'd just sit inside an all too brief moment of respite and envision her smile. Nothing else, just her smile. The vision never failed to warm him.

The ease with which he'd gone from committed bachelor to committed lover astounded him.

What was even more astonishing was that, when confronted with the situation, he didn't suddenly feel like a drowning man desperately trying to swim for shore. This feeling pervading all through him wasn't a trap, it was a haven.

And he wanted it to continue.

He wanted, he knew, to have Jolene in his life for the long haul. He wanted for them to be a family. Jolene and Amanda, Tommy and him.

The fact that he had always been against this sort of thing no longer meant anything to him, carried no weight. Apparently his commitment phobia had come to an end, not with a bang, but with the tiniest of whispers.

And he couldn't have been happier about it.

The only problem was, the one person he needed to share this with eluded him.

He'd been back at the hospital for two days now.

In that time, despite the fact that he knew she was on duty, he hadn't managed to cross Jolene's path. Every time he tried to find her, a nurse or orderly would tell him that he'd "just missed her."

What made it really odd was that she wasn't at home when he called and even though he'd left her messages, she didn't return them.

He began to wonder if he'd somehow done something to offend her without realizing it.

Wouldn't that be a kick in the head, he mused. All his life, he hadn't cared about maintaining relationships and they'd been there, waiting on him, ripe for the picking. Now he'd found someone he wanted to be with and she seemed to be avoiding him for some reason.

"Hey, Dr. Mac, the lady you're looking for is just coming out of Trauma Three," Jorge called out to him as he walked by.

Mac tossed the file he'd just picked up on the nurse's desk and rounded the corner, going down the corridor to Trauma Room Three.

He spotted her hurrying away from the room.

"Hey, Nurse DeLuca," Mac called out teasingly. When she didn't stop, he picked up his pace to catch up to her. "Didn't you hear me calling you?"

What the hell was going on? he wondered. Taking her arm, he pulled her over to the side, out of the way of foot traffic and gurneys.

"No," she lied. She'd been playing hide-and-seek in the corridors for the last two days, but she'd known that eventually her luck was going to play itself out. She wasn't up to this, she thought, even as she offered him a polite, impersonal smile. "How's Tommy doing?"

Something *was* wrong. "Fine, but I didn't corner you to talk about Tommy."

She shrugged out of his grasp. "Mac, I don't have time to talk."

She'd never called him Mac before. He looked at her, his eyes pinning her far more effectively than his grip had. "You're harder to get a hold of than Tommy's stepfather was."

"I've been busy."

He put his hand up in front of her, barring her way. "That was his excuse, too. You know, if I didn't know any better, I'd say you were avoiding me."

She ducked under his arm, then continued walking the way she'd been. "That's ridiculous."

Turning on his heel, he followed her down the corridor. "Then why haven't you returned any of my calls?"

She was aware that people were looking at them. She lowered her voice. "I told you, I've been busy. Am busy. Look, maybe we can talk later."

Then, without waiting for him to answer, she hurried off, leaving him to stand in her wake and wonder what had suddenly gone wrong.

Mac was waiting for her outside the staff lounge at the end of her shift. As she opened the door, he fell into place beside her. "Okay, this is later."

It took her a second to recover. Lost in thought, he'd startled her.

Hardening herself to what she knew was ahead, knowing that if she let it slide, if she let her guard down, she was going to pay an even greater price than she was right at this second, she told him coolly, "I have to go home, MacKenzie."

Formal. He didn't know whether he should be worried or not. "Fine, I'll come with you."

Jolene stopped abruptly. That was the last thing she wanted. For him to come home with her. Because if he did, she might just break down and tell him. And then suffer as she watched him ease himself away from her.

She was going to call the shots, not him. "No."

None of this was making any sense to him. "Is this the brush-off?"

Was that the sound of his ego taking offense that she heard? Her eyes narrowed. "Oh, right, you have no experience with that, do you? You're usually the brusher, not the brushee."

"What the hell are you talking about?" When she turned away from him rather than answer, he grabbed her by the arm, forcing her to look at him. Anger warred with a sense of panic formed in the pit of his stomach. "Wait, I don't care what you're talking about. I don't want to go down this road any further, I just want this to be over."

She felt herself getting deliberately belligerent. "Oh, so what I feel doesn't count."

Where had that come from? "I didn't say that." He held her in place, his hands on her shoulders. He wasn't about to let her leave until they had this straightened out. "Jolene, what's wrong with you?"

She pushed his hands away defiantly, her chin up in an unspoken challenge. "Nothing. Nothing's wrong with me. I've just decided not to wait around for you to walk out on me, that's all. So I'm the one who's doing the walking.''

He was hearing the words, but they weren't making any sense to him. ''So you're telling me that you want to break up because you don't want to break up.''

''Yes.'' She shook her head. ''No.'' And then she blew out an angry breath. ''You're confusing me.''

''Well, that makes two of us.'' Losing his temper wasn't going to solve anything. And neither was giving in to the panic gnawing away at his belly. Mac tried again. ''Listen to me, I don't want to break up, I want to cement together.''

He was making it sound like a big joke. Well, none of it was funny to her. ''That's what you say now, but—''

Maybe she wasn't listening. ''That's what I say forever.''

''You don't know the meaning of the word.'' She tried to leave again, but he wouldn't let her.

''Forever,'' he repeated, then said, ''For all eternity. The opposite of never.''

She recalled hearing somewhere that Mac had a photographic memory. That would account for why he probably never forgot a phone number. ''That's from the dictionary.''

He lifted a shoulder and then let it fall. ''Works for me.''

She couldn't stand here arguing with him anymore. It was ripping her apart. But she knew that if he found out about the aneurysm and then walked out on her, she wouldn't be able to stand it. This way was better.

Even though it hurt like hell right now.

Jolene pushed his arm away and hurried from him. "I have to get home, Mac. Leave me alone."

"What did you do to her?"

Mac turned around to see Howard Monroe standing behind him. "I didn't do anything to her, but she just shot me at close range."

Howard smoothed down his drooping navy-and-white bowtie with his thumb and forefinger. His expression was compassionate when he looked at him. "Why don't you come by my office for a cup of coffee?"

Maybe letting her go to cool off like this wasn't the right idea. Mac shook his head. "I don't want a cup of coffee, Howard, I need to go after her—" He stopped, surprised when the surgeon took hold of his arm. Mac looked at him quizzically.

"Trust me, you'll want this cup of coffee."

Mac had always liked the older man, although he'd thought him a little eccentric. But right now, he was in no mood to indulge him. Still, if he ran after Jolene in her present mood, who knew what would be said?

"All right."

Mac walked in silence beside the white-haired man to the rear of the hospital. He was lost in his thoughts, trying to understand what had just happened.

The small office where Monroe saw patients at the hospital was located next to the MRI lab. He'd been in the office since 1966. There was clutter everywhere, held together by a layer of dust.

Picking up a handful of folders from the small table, Howard cleared off the surface. "Sit down," he said, depositing the folders in the corner on an extra chair.

Mac looked over his shoulder toward the doorway. He was wasting time. "I—"

"Sit down," Howard instructed more firmly. He picked up the coffeepot from the small burner he used and filled a cup.

Mac frowned, looking at his watch. "I've got a baby-sitter at home who charges double-time after five."

"You can afford it." Howard placed the cup of inky-black coffee in front of him. "So how's Jolene doing these days?"

It was an odd question, coming out of the blue like this. It wasn't as if he and Monroe had ever had close, intimate conversations. Theirs ran along the lines of discussing new operating techniques and upcoming medications.

Mac looked at him. "Why are you asking?"

Howard behaved as if it his inquiry was the most natural thing in the world. "I always take an interest in my patients."

He stared at the other man. "Jolene's your patient? Why? What did she come to see you for?"

Howard raised a brow, his kindly eyes meeting Mac's. *Poor kid's been through the wringer,* he thought. "You know I can't discuss that."

That was under normal circumstances. The circumstances here weren't normal. They were about Jolene. "All right, show me her file."

Crossing to the file cabinet, Howard pulled out a large folder and held it aloft. "You mean this one?" He shook his head when Mac reached for it. "That's not ethical, either."

Mac was just about at the end of his tether. Something was wrong with Jolene and he needed to know what. "Howard, the hell with ethics."

"No." Howard's voice was very calm, very soft. Someone had once said that he'd be the last man to lose his head in the middle of a disaster. "Without ethics, patients wouldn't trust us and then we couldn't do our jobs. It's part of our code. Just like washing our hands."

What the hell was he going on about? Mac thought impatiently. Right or wrong, he fought the urge just to take the folder out of the neurosurgeon's hands.

Howard placed the folder down on the desk and regarded his hands. "You know, I think I forgot to wash my hands after my last patient. Can't be too careful these days." He winked, as if talking to himself. "I'll be back in a few minutes, Mac. Feel free to drink your coffee while I'm gone."

When he returned several minutes later, the office was empty. Mac's coffee cup was full.

"Nobody takes the time to enjoy a good cup of coffee anymore," Howard murmured.

Moving the cup aside, he took the folder and returned it to the file cabinet, then sat down. He picked up the cup and held it in both hands, savoring the aroma. He hated seeing a good cup of coffee go to waste.

Mac called the sitter on his cell phone while he was driving, checking to make sure she could stay with Tommy until he got home. The woman, Adriana, was only too happy to remain. The mother of three grown children, she missed having children to look after.

His mind was at least at rest on that score, Mac focused on the battle that he knew lay ahead. He was having trouble keeping his temper in check. He felt slighted and discarded.

Squeaking through yellow lights that were about to turn red, he made it to Jolene's door less than fifteen minutes later. When she didn't answer the doorbell, he knocked. Hard.

Still nothing.

"If you don't open this door, Jolene," he yelled, not caring who heard, "I'm going to break in through the window."

That got results. Just as he was stripping off his jacket, the front door opened.

Jolene glared at him. Why couldn't he leave her alone? Why did he have to make this even more difficult than it already was?

"I can't afford a new window."

"I was counting on that." Not waiting for an invitation, he walked in. "Where's Amanda?"

"She's at my mother's." She'd asked her mother to take the little girl for the night, needing some time alone. She still hadn't been able to bring herself to tell her mother about the aneurysm, but she could tell that her mother suspected something was wrong.

Everything was just a finite matter of time.

Mac turned on her without warning. "What the hell is wrong with you?"

She shouldn't have let him push his way in. Now she was going to have to make him leave. "I told you, I don't want to see you anymore."

He wasn't about to get into that waltz again. "I meant why didn't you tell me?"

"I just did—"

She was playing dumb and he didn't like it. It didn't suit her. "Goddamn it, woman, why didn't you tell me about the aneurysm?"

She paled. No one knew about that. Only Dr. Monroe and her. "Who told you?"

He wasn't about to go into an explanation about cups of coffee and hand washing. "No one told me, I just found out." She was doing it again, trying to distract him. "And that's beside the point."

Her temper flared. This was supposed to be a secret. "No, it is the point—"

He took hold of her shoulders, as if that could somehow make her see reason. "No, what is the point is that you didn't trust me to tell me about this."

Trust. The last time she'd trusted someone to be there for her, he'd disappeared, leaving her emotionally alone. Leaving her with a broken heart. That wasn't going to happen again.

"So you could do what?" she demanded. "Start a chorus of 'Good-night Irene' and make a quick retreat? I didn't need that on top of everything else." She felt hysteria bubbling up within her. Why couldn't he just be a gentleman and leave? Why did he have to keep chipping away at her like this, until there was nothing left? "What I have or don't have is none of your business."

Did she actually believe what she was saying? "Don't you get it yet? You are my business."

"Right," she retorted. "For how long?"

The woman had a short memory for someone so bright. "Are you asking me to recite the definition of forever again?"

"No," she said wearily, waving him away, "and I don't want to hear any other lies, either. I'm not up to it." She turned away, rubbing her brow. "Now just go, I have a headache."

When she heard no movement, she turned around. He was exactly where she'd left him.

"I'm not going."

Why was he doing this to her? Why was he torturing her like this, getting her to believe that he really was one of the good guys when she knew there was no such animal. "I can have you removed. I can get a restraining order."

Mac looked at her pointedly. "Now who's running away?"

Tears were pushing their way through her system, threatening to spill out. She didn't want to cry in front of him.

She had no choice. The tears came anyway, despite all her attempts to block them. She had no say, even in this.

"I don't want to be left," she told him. "I want to walk away on my own. I have my pride."

So that was it. She was afraid. Well, so was he. Afraid of losing her. "Pride's a pretty cold thing to curl up with at night."

She sniffed, wiping away tears with the back of her hand. "But it's better than nothing."

"How about better than something?" She looked at him. "Is having your pride better than having someone in your life who loves you?"

He was being unfair, she thought. She didn't have the strength to fight him off, not when all she wanted was for him to hold her, to make everything better.

But he couldn't. He could only make things worse. She'd let herself believe him and then he'd walk away, the way Matt had.

"I don't know. I haven't had that happen yet. I thought it did, but then I was rudely awakened."

"Not every man is like your ex-husband," he told her patiently. "Not even every doctor is like him."

"But you were," she insisted. "You are." Now she was the one who wasn't being fair, but she was fighting for her survival now. "The only difference is that you never got married."

He resented the comparison to a man he had come to loathe on principle, but he held his reaction in check. "And I was always honest. I never told a woman she was my one true love."

She had to give him that. She knew his reputation. There had never been any promises from him. They'd only lived in the moment. "No—"

He cut her off before she could continue. "Until now."

Jolene stared at him. She'd misheard. There was no other explanation. "What?"

He leaned over and whispered the words in her ear. "Until now," he repeated.

She drew back as if he'd just burned her flesh. "You're saying you love me."

"Yes." He moved to take her into his arms.

Jolene sidestepped him, refusing to let her guard down. What he felt wasn't love. "That's pity," she insisted.

He looked at her incredulously. Was she out of her mind?

"Why the hell should I pity you? If anything, I

pity me for standing here, banging my head against the wall, putting up with a tongue-lashing. I can't think of a single reason to pity you except maybe that you're just too stubborn to see beyond your memory. Too stubborn to see that history is *not* doomed to repeat itself if you make the right choice.''

He was wearing her down and she didn't want him to. "Meaning you."

Mac touched her face. "Yeah."

She curled her fingers, digging her nails into her palms, trying to focus on that instead of melting.

"You said yourself you can't stand to see a child in pain. You've just broadened your base, that's all. You're not a self-centered bastard, you're a good, kind man when it comes to the downtrodden. I know that. But once this—this *thing* is behind me, then maybe you'll rethink your feelings, come to your senses and go on to the next woman."

How did he make her understand? "I'm not interested in you as the disease of the week, or the month, or my cause of the year, Jolene. I am just interested in you, period."

She held her head. The headaches rarely stopped now. This one had been plaguing her all day and was now at its apex. "I can't process this right now. My head feels like it's coming off."

Though he wanted to press her for a decision, for a commitment, Mac backed away. Nothing would be settled tonight.

It felt strange, he thought. He'd run from commitment all of his adult life only to have someone withhold it from him now that he wanted it.

There was irony in that. He knew a few who would

call it poetic justice. But this wasn't about him. It was about Jolene. Which meant that his feelings had to be shelved for the time being.

"When are you having the surgery?" There hadn't been any indication of that in the notes he'd read in her file.

Jolene began to shake her head, then stopped. The pain was too great. "I don't know. I haven't set a date." She saw him stride to the phone and pick the receiver up. "What are you doing?"

He was already pressing buttons. "Calling Howard at home to set one up."

She put her hand on the cradle, disconnecting him. "You can't do that. It's my life."

His fingers curled around the receiver, channeling his anger. "Wrong again. It's not your life. It's Amanda's and your mother's. And mine," he insisted firmly. "No matter how much you want to be, you're not in this alone."

She *didn't* want to be in this alone. She just was. "You're hurting my head."

"You're hurting my heart. We're even." He looked at her expectantly, his eyes indicating the receiver. "Now can I make the call?"

"No." She took the receiver from him, then sighed. "I'll make the call."

He stood beside her as she dialed.

Chapter Sixteen

Erika looked up from the coloring book spread out before her. She was helping Amanda choose a color for the clown's feet. Tommy was beside her on the sofa, carefully examining the crayons in the box before rendering his opinion. When he offered her an orange crayon, Amanda took it from him solemnly, her impatience melting.

Mac was pacing around the room like a caged tiger that was searching for a way out.

Leaving the children with each other, Erika walked up behind him and placed a hand on his shoulder. "She'll be all right."

He covered her hand with his, silently thanking the woman for the comfort she was offering. He wasn't used to this, wasn't used to waiting, to not knowing. Not doing. Time dragged on longer when you couldn't do anything about it.

Mac turned and smiled at Jolene's mother. "I'm supposed to be the one telling you that."

"I know." She lifted her shoulder in a half shrug. "Just in case you forgot, I thought I'd say it out loud for both of us." And then anxiety pushed forward, getting the better of her. She looked at her watch. "Is it supposed to be taking this long?"

They hadn't exceeded the customary surgical time range, even though it felt like several eternities had gone by since they'd watched the operating room doors close on Jolene and filed into the lounge to wait for word.

Mac went into his best physician's mode, realizing now from this vantage point how little comfort the words actually were. "It's not something you want to rush through. They want to make sure that nothing vital gets affected while they're draining the aneurysm."

He'd already explained it to her earlier, before Jolene had gone in for the surgery. The patient remained awake through the operation and the surgeon proceeds cautiously, asking a battery of questions for every minute movement that was executed.

It had been just two days since he'd stormed into Jolene's house. Two days since he'd fully realized just how much she meant to him.

He'd never felt so helpless, so useless.

Shoving his hands into his pockets, he began to pace around the lounge again, grateful that there was no one else in it beside Erika and the kids. He would have preferred leaving Tommy with the sitter, but the boy had begged to come once he'd discovered that Jolene was having surgery. When Tommy continued to plead, Mac had given in and brought him along. Under the pending circumstances, he thought it only fitting.

He realized by the look on Erika's face that Tommy had asked him a question and was waiting for an answer.

Crossing to the boy, he squatted down to his level. "I'm sorry, what?"

Tommy took a deep breath. "Is her doctor as good a doctor as you are?"

Mac laughed, touched at the boy's obvious adulation. "Better. He's at the top of his field. None better." The testimony was supposed to comfort Erika and Tommy. He clung to the words himself as if they were a life raft he was using to navigate his way through the rapids.

Tommy's face was a wreath of smiles. "Then Jo's gonna be okay."

Mac hugged the boy to him. Who was comforting whom? "Yes, she's going to be okay."

She had to be, Mac silently insisted. He wasn't going to allow his thoughts to go in any other direction. Jolene was going to pull through. Any other possibility didn't enter into it. Because it just couldn't happen.

"Why don't you go over there and help Amanda? I think she needs you to pick another color for her."

Tommy sighed. "Women." But he was obviously happy to be of service.

"My sentiments exactly," Mac said under his breath. He'd been much better off when it was a matter of a multitude of women rather than a single woman. Because now his stomach was completely tied up in knots. Just like his heart.

Howard Monroe didn't come looking for them until another half hour had passed. The doctor walked into the lounge still wearing his scrubs, his mask at half-mast around his neck.

Erika froze when she saw him. Mac made it across the length of the room in three strides, taking Howard's arm, as if that somehow assured him of the right answer to the question he put to him. "Well?"

Howard smiled, nodding. "Yes, she will be." His gaze took in both mother and worried significant other. "Jolene came through with flying colors." Howard thought of sitting down, then decided against it. If he sat, he'd never get up and he needed to change. "Lucky we went in when we did. The aneurysm gave every sign of rupturing. As it was, we got it all. She'll be up and flying in no time."

Tears in her eyes, Erika hugged the surgeon. "Oh thank you, thank you."

"Entirely my pleasure." Howard looked at Mac over Erika's shoulder. "By the way, she's asking for you."

The news surprised him. He would have thought Jolene would have asked after her mother or Amanda. "Me?"

Howard nodded, removing the mask's ties from around his neck. "I think she mumbled something about a damn bastard." A genial smile curved his mouth. "I figured that had to be you."

Mac looked at Erika uncertainly. It was enough that he knew Jolene was all right. He could wait now. "Her mother should—"

"No," Erika told him. "You go in first." She gave him a little push to set him moving. "I'll stay out here with the children and celebrate."

Grateful, Mac began to hurry out, then doubled back and brushed a kiss on the older woman's cheek. No words were necessary.

Erika smiled. "I see what she sees in you. Actually I saw it first." She shooed him out. "Go, tell her we were all out here, rooting for her."

He barely heard the end of her sentence.

Very quietly, Mac made his way into the recovery room. There were times when the area was teeming with beds, all separated from each other only by the curtains that hung from the ceiling and served as temporary walls.

But the load was light today. The last patient had just been taken up to his room. Jolene's was the only bed in the dimly lit enclosure.

As he approached her, Jolene appeared to be groggy, but awake. Mac's heart constricted looking at her.

Just thinking of what he might have lost at the very moment when he'd realized he'd found it...

He leaned his hands on the railings, marveling at how fragile she seemed. And how perfect, despite the bandage over half her head. "Hi."

She gazed up at him, vaguely aware that she had to look terrible.

"Hi." The word all but croaked out of her parched throat. She'd done a lot of talking in the operating room. That and the surgery had left her pretty much exhausted.

Mac nodded toward the entrance. "Your mother and the kids are outside."

"I have kids?" she asked wryly. "When did that happen? I thought I just had one."

"Amanda and Tommy. He insisted on coming once he knew about the surgery. Felt it was his duty since you were there for his." For the first time, Mac's tongue felt heavy. He was just so grateful she was all right.

"I remember," she murmured.

"Your mother let me come in first." He glanced again toward the entrance, thinking that perhaps Jolene might rather have seen her mother in his stead. "Nice lady."

"I always thought so." She blew out a breath slowly, then dragged another in. Breathing was taking concentrated effort. "What I didn't think...was that you'd be here."

He took her hand in his. How did he make her understand? "When are you going to stop underestimating me?" A grin played on his lips. "Besides, bald women turn me on."

She closed her eyes, thinking of what she had to look like. Too bad Halloween wasn't around the corner. She'd be all ready. "Don't remind me."

She'd never looked more beautiful to him. "It's just a section, not your whole head."

"Great," she sighed, then took another deep breath. Her eyes felt like lead. "I'll start a new style."

Mac stroked her hand. "Just as long as you're around to start it, that's all that counts." Was this happiness he was feeling inside? It hurt, he thought.

It hurt to be this happy. "You're a lucky woman, they got it just in time. All of it."

Jolene tried to nod and found that any movement hurt. This was going to be slow going. But then, she wasn't going anywhere.

"That's good."

She vaguely remembered that the surgeon had said something along those lines, but everything was getting blurry now. She just wanted to sleep.

"Now it's time for me to get lucky."

She opened her eyes wider as his words registered. Well, at least he was being honest with her. What did a man like him want with a half-bald temporary invalid? "New prospect?"

She'd misunderstood. He shouldn't have joked. "New venue." Mac collected himself, looking for words, serious words. "This isn't exactly the most romantic setting, but seeing as how we've all been given a second chance here, it'll do. Jolene, will you marry me?"

When she didn't answer, he looked down at her and realized that she'd fallen asleep.

Frustrated, Mac blew out a breath. Okay, so this was just dress rehearsal.

She was someplace else.

Jolene peeled her upper eyelashes away from her lower ones, trying to see. Trying to focus beyond the haze.

This wasn't the Recovery Room anymore.

When had that happened?

Or was the other a dream and she'd been here all

along? She could have sworn that Mac had asked her to marry him.

Right, like that would ever happen.

What *had* the anesthesiologist given her to make her groggy like that?

Her eyes were closed again. She was looking at the inside of her lids. With effort, she opened them again. There was someone beside her.

Holding her hand.

A nurse, probably.

How about that, she thought, giddy, the nurse needs a nurse.

Jolene took a deep breath, filling her lungs so she could talk.

"I'm alive." The words were said to no one in particular and to the world at large.

"Yes, I know."

The deep voice rippled all around her.

A male nurse?

No, wait, she knew that voice. It filled her head and her dreams. It was in the last one she remembered hearing before...

For the third time, she opened her eyes. And focused in on—

"Mac."

He grinned at her. "You were expecting Santa Claus?"

"No." He'd come. He hadn't bailed out, he'd come. Happiness poured through her veins, chasing away the anesthetic. Making her feel alive. Groggy, but alive. Very alive. "I guess I fell asleep."

"I guess you did." This was something they were going to talk about every anniversary, he decided, how she'd fallen asleep during his proposal. He'd never let her forget. "Right in the middle."

She didn't quite follow. "Of surgery?"

"Of my proposal."

She blinked, trying to dispel the last bit of grogginess from her bruised brain. "No one told me I'd be delirious after surgery."

His grin deepened. "You're not."

She was not about to let herself get carried away, no matter what her insides insisted on doing. "Then why am I hearing the word proposal?"

"Maybe because I said it." His eyes held hers, his voice dropping. "Maybe because I did it."

"Do it again." It was almost a dare. She was afraid to believe him.

Mac took her hand in both of his. "Jolene, will you marry me?"

She couldn't be hearing right. This was Harrison MacKenzie, Southern California's leading playboy. The eternal bachelor. The only thing he proposed were illicit liaisons.

"Did I sleep right through to April Fools'?"

"No." She needed to be convinced. He could understand that. He had, too. But now, nothing was going to unconvince him. "Jolene, I never thought I'd say those words, never thought I'd want to get married to anyone. I know that maintaining a marriage is going to take harder work than becoming a doctor ever did, but I'm willing to work at it, as long as it's with you."

She had to say yes. He intended to keep at her until she did. Because he knew she wanted it as much as he did. They were just both afraid. Or had been.

"Willing to do anything to keep you in my life. I want us to be a family, Jolene. You and me, Amanda and Tommy—and your mother." He hoped that would clinch the deal. He was willing to do anything.

She ached too much for this to be a dream. Jolene pressed her lips together. "This is a lot to spring on a person who just lost half her hair."

"I can wait. You're not going anywhere." He looked at her significantly. "Neither am I."

She'd been completely dried out by the surgery. Otherwise, she knew there would have been tears in her eyes. "So you're serious."

"Never more."

She lay there, studying his face. Realizing that sometimes, miracles did happen. "Bald women really turn you on."

He laughed. "Singular. Bald 'woman.'" He picked up her hand again and held it in his, his eyes intent on her face. "This bald woman."

He meant it. She could feel it. Was it possible to feel this much happiness and not explode? "I guess then I shouldn't deprive you, should I?"

Mac moved his head from side to side. "Wouldn't be right."

A glint entered her eyes and he knew that he was home free. "Does this mean I'll have to keep shaving half my head?"

"You can do anything you like—after you say I do."

"Can't beat a deal like that."

"I'm counting on it."

Just as he leaned over to kiss her, Jolene placed her fingers to his lips. He looked at her quizzically.

"And this isn't some postoperative thing with you? You don't have some condition that compels you to propose to every woman being wheeled into recovery, do you?"

He tried to keep a straight face as he crossed his heart. "Never happened before."

"Then I guess the answer's yes."

He arched a brow. "You guess?"

"I know," she corrected. "I'm willing to give you a try." And then, because he'd told her, she added seriously, "I do love you, Harrison."

Somehow, though he'd always disliked the name, hearing her say it made everything that much more intimate. "We're going to do more than try, Jolene. We're going to make it."

She smiled just before he kissed her, echoing his phrase. "I'm counting on it."

* * * * *

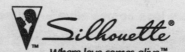

If you enjoyed what you just read,
then we've got an offer you can't resist!

Take 2 bestselling
love stories FREE!
Plus get a FREE surprise gift!

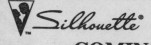

COMING NEXT MONTH